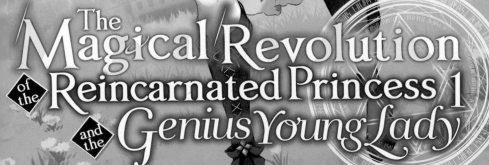

The Magical Revolution
of the Reincarnated Princess 1
and the Genius Young Lady

CHARACTERS

Euphyllia Magenta (15 years old)

The daughter of Duke Magenta, formerly engaged to Anisphia's brother, Algard. A prodigy who excels in her studies, magic, politics, and the martial arts, she is also graced with an unrivaled serene personality.

Anisphia Wynn Palettia (17 years old)

First Princess of the Kingdom of Palettia. So famed for her eccentricity that she has become known as "Princess Peculiar." Although she's never been able to use magic herself, she devotes her days to her own brand of magical research, magicology, aiming to imitate the effects of magic.

Lainie Cyan (15 years old)

The daughter of a commoner elevated to the rank of baron. Despite her humble origins, she has succeeded in attracting the attention of the sons of several influential nobles at the Aristocratic Academy, and she has stirred up considerable trouble…

Ilia Coral (27 years old)

Anisphia's personal maid. Although a servant, she watches over Anisphia like an older sister. She was saved by Anisphia in the past and is deeply loyal to her.

...I laid Lady Anis down on the ground, placing her head on my lap as I stared into her face. She was beaming with joy—and relief, too.

"...I've never let anyone rest their head on my lap, not even Prince Algard."

" "

...

"Euphie... Let's hunt a dragon!"

"If that's what you want, I'll stick with you forever."

CONTENTS

001 OPENING

CHAPTER 1
019 The Reincarnated Princess Can't Brake Suddenly

CHAPTER 2
045 The Reincarnated Princess Makes a House Call

CHAPTER 3
073 The Reincarnated Princess's Magicology Lesson

CHAPTER 4
093 Like Picturing a Rainbow

CHAPTER 5
125 The Reincarnated Princess Still Yearns for Magic

183 ENDING

205 AFTERWORD

Author
Piero Karasu

Illustration
Yuri Kisaragi

The Magical Revolution
of the Reincarnated Princess
and the Genius Young Lady

1

Piero Karasu

Illustration by Yuri Kisaragi

YEN ON

New York

The Magical Revolution of the Reincarnated Princess and the Genius Young Lady 1

Piero Karasu

Translation by Haydn Trowell
Cover art by Yuri Kisaragi

TENSEI OJO TO TENSAI REIJO NO MAHO KAKUMEI Vol.1
© Piero Karasu, Yuri Kisaragi 2020
First published in Japan in 2020 by KADOKAWA CORPORATION, Tokyo. English translation rights arranged with KADOKAWA CORPORATION, Tokyo through TUTTLE-MORI AGENCYI, INC., Tokyo.

English translation © 2022 by Yen Press, LLC

Yen On
150 West 30th Street, 19th Floor
New York, NY 10001

Visit us at yenpress.com | facebook.com/yenpress | twitter.com/yenpress
yenpress.tumblr.com | instagram.com/yenpress

First Yen On Edition: March 2022

Yen On is an imprint of Yen Press, LLC.
The Yen On name and logo are trademarks of Yen Press, LLC.

Library of Congress Cataloging-in-Publication Data
Names: Karasu, Piero, author. | Kisaragi, Yuri, illustrator. | Trowell, Haydn, translator.
Title: The magical revolution of the reincarnated princess and the genius young lady / Piero Karasu ; illustration by Yuri Kisaragi ; translation by Haydn Trowell.
Other titles: Tensei ojo to tensai reijo no maho kakumei. English
Description: First Yen On edition. | New York, NY : Yen On, 2022.
Identifiers: LCCN 2021060085 | ISBN 9781975337803 (v. 1 ; trade paperback) |
    ISBN 9781975337827 (v. 2 ; trade paperback) | ISBN 9781975337841 (v. 3 ; trade paperback)
Subjects: CYAC: Magic —Fiction. | Princesses —Fiction. | Reincarnation —Fiction. | LCGFT: Fantasy. |
    Light novels.
Classification: LCC PZ7.1.K3626 Mag 2022 | DDC [Fic] —dc23
LC record available at https://lccn.loc.gov/2021060085

ISBNs: 978-1-9753-3780-3 (paperback)
        978-1-9753-3781-0 (ebook)

10 9 8 7 6 5 4 3 2 1

WOR

Printed in the United States of America

OPENING

This is the tale of a princess from a certain kingdom.

A tale that begins when our princess, having always harbored a deep yearning for magic, found herself regaining her memories of a previous life.

At times she wielded her influence and at other times her charm, and she was always in pursuit of the alluring power of magic.

This is how her tale begins...

* * *

I've always loved the word *magic*. It has a way of making people happy, of putting a smile on their faces. I adore magic because it's always out of reach. It's not possible in reality. If I could have any wish come true, it would be to wield magic myself. I wanted nothing more than that.

Then, by some sudden twist of fate, I remembered the details of a *past life*.

My name is Anisphia Wynn Palettia, and I am the First Princess of the Kingdom of Palettia.

It happened when I was five years old, staring up at the sky in a daydream.

If only I had magic, I would be able to fly, I had thought—and that was the moment it happened. I don't know exactly why.

Why had that thought crossed my mind? I asked myself, just as memories of a past life came flowing back to me as easily as some small detail I had simply forgotten.

It was like the pieces of a jigsaw puzzle falling into place. As if I had rediscovered something that had been missing from my whole existence. That day was a turning point.

Those memories of my past life were nothing if not filled with mystery. One after another, they came back to me—airplanes soaring through the sky, asphalt roads, cars speeding across those roads, and other products of civilization that struck me as so commonplace.

But such things were all unknown to me as well. There were no "airplanes" or "cars" in the world in which I now dwelled. The only things soaring through the sky here were birds and monsters. The roads weren't made of asphalt, and they were traversed by horse-drawn carriages, not cars. In my past life, aristocrats and nobles had been no more than characters in stories, but here I was, a royal princess myself.

As all these memories rushed back to me, a word escaped my lips: "…Uh-oh."

I was at such a loss that I began to fret. I mean, ever since those memories of my past life first came back to me, I was finding their influence on my thoughts, beliefs, and values overtaking my upbringing as Princess Anisphia.

I was aware of my obligations as a member of the royal family, of the dignity and poise expected of me as an aristocrat. I was always conscious of that. And yet my sense of connection to those ideals had faded. In my previous life, the world had kept on spinning even without nobles. When I thought about it that way, I started feeling unsettled, as though I was somehow at odds with my own royal upbringing. I knew I was the strange one here, that I was the one who was out of place. And yet it was because I was aware of all this that I didn't want to change what seemed to me the appropriate way of things. Nothing good would come from reviving these memories now.

"Well, no matter!"

I decided not to worry about it. After all, I was only five. My values would inevitably change with time and experience. Maybe I would be able to manage? I was overly optimistic back then, thinking I could put off the issue for later. I was more concerned about fulfilling the desires that were within reach now rather than worrying about whatever problems might lie ahead.

"Right! Because *this* world is filled with magic!"

In this world, magic wasn't just something featured in fairy tales and fantasy stories, but it actually, truly existed.

People could command fire, manipulate water, steer the wind, and direct the earth. I couldn't comment on what theory or logic lay behind those abilities, but just bearing witness to it all made my heart do cartwheels.

If *I* could wield magic, maybe I would be able to fly—because magic *did* exist. I just couldn't stop thinking about it. My imagination was soaring; my heart was racing!

"There's no time like the present, right?"

With renewed determination, I clenched my fists and dashed out from my room as fast as my feet could carry me. As I charged through the corridors of the royal palace and turned a corner, I suddenly brushed past a young lady, a maid in the service of the palace. I ducked my head slightly and tried to sneak past her, when—

"Y-Your Highness?! You mustn't run in the corridors!" She grabbed ahold of me from behind, unwilling to let me escape.

I struggled a little, but she had caught me easily. After all, I was just a child.

She was putting all her strength into holding me, which meant I would have no chance of getting away. I surrendered myself, letting my muscles relax. When I glanced up, I realized that hers was a familiar face.

"Oh, Ilia? I'm sorry. I'm in a bit of a hurry."

"Even so, you mustn't run through the castle like that."

"Ugh, so cruel…"

Escape seemed impossible, so I resigned myself to my fate. Seeing my resistance fade, Ilia lowered me back down to my feet, before crouching down to meet me at eye level.

"Why are you in such a hurry, Princess?"

"I need to make a petition to my father!"

"A—a petition…?"

"Yes! I want him to let me learn magic!"

"…Ah, I see. Magic…"

I had answered her without hesitation, but for some reason, a look of consternation passed over her face.

"Ilia. I want to learn magic."

"It *is* good to have ambitions. But where has this come from all of a sudden? Why are you so interested in magic again?"

"Because I want to fly!"

"Huh?"

"I want to fly!"

"With magic?"

"Yes! I want to fly!"

Judging by her expression, Ilia had no idea what I was talking about. That was understandable. As far as I was aware, the notion of using magic as a means of flight was unheard of.

"That's just one of the things I want to do! I could do so much good with magic! I could use it to scare off villains and help people!"

"I see, I see. That *is* a noble dream, isn't it? But His Majesty is very busy. So how about I relate your request later, while you go back to your room for now?"

"Ngh… I suppose so. I'll allow you to ask him in my stead, then, Ilia!"

"Thank you, Your Highness." Ilia gave her chest a slight thump, as if to say it would be no trouble at all.

She had a full bosom—and a beautiful face, too. Was it because she was so attractive that she had been employed to serve here in the castle?

Well, there was nothing else I could do, so I allowed her to escort me back to my room. I tried to focus on my memories as Anisphia, but today's lessons were over. That being the case, I instead occupied myself by poking around my room, but that only ended up amplifying my sense of anticipation.

Looking back now, that moment was the beginning of what would become my new life.

I'll do it! I told myself. *I'll become a magic user one day!*

* * *

After the young girl's awakening, time passed.

The Kingdom of Palettia was a great nation whose development was fueled by magic. In this country, the government ran an academy for nobles and members of the royal family, the Royal Aristocratic Academy of Palettia. The academy, welcoming exchange students even from far-flung lands, was considered a microcosm of high society at large.

Of course, the academy was supposed to be a place of learning. However, no matter how much the instructors might intend to encourage their students to focus on their grades without regard to their respective social statuses, nobles were nobles, and royalty was royalty.

It was common for students of high status to gain followers around them, while those of low status were forever at risk of losing their positions in the academy's social hierarchy if they failed to curry favor with their more elevated peers.

Moreover, any attempts by a student's parents to intervene in their children's quarrels could easily lead to further disputes. For this reason, the Royal Aristocratic Academy of Palettia was a closed world of sorts.

Well. Today was an auspicious day for the academy. The final exams for the soon-to-be graduates would almost be complete, and a party was about to be held to celebrate their achievements and all the hard work they had put into their studies.

There was even an orchestra playing refined, graceful music as the students mingled. It was a resplendent gathering, ripe with anticipation and, at least on the surface, full of pageantry and splendor...but then everything changed.

* * *

"I hereby declare that I am breaking off my engagement to Euphyllia Magenta!" a loud and powerful voice announced.

The voice belonged to Algard Von Palettia, heir apparent to the Kingdom of Palettia.

His platinum-colored hair, like burnished rays of sunlight, was a hue often found among the royal family, while his blue eyes, despite their gentle tint, possessed a strong sense of will.

And the prince had just announced the annulment of our engagement. With a single sentence, the magnificent party had been transformed all at once from celebration and revelry into a court of impeachment.

I—Euphyllia Magenta—could only stare back at him in astonishment. My eyes widened in shame, and I bit my lip, unable to speak. All I could do was watch on in disbelief.

After all, I was the daughter of the duke of Magenta, of the Kingdom of Palettia. My whole life until now had been preparing me for my future role as the betrothed of the future king...

I struggled to speak. "...Your Highness. Why are you doing this?"

I certainly wasn't the perfect fiancée, and I knew for a fact that Algard didn't hold much affection for me.

But even so, our betrothal had been ordained by the king himself. Our engagement was necessary for the sake of the country. And so I had always honestly believed that, someday, Prince Algard would understand.

To tell the truth, I felt no spark of romance for him, either, but I had sworn to myself that I would fulfill my role and support the man who would one day take on the responsibilities of king. That was the role I was supposed to play for my country as his bride-to-be.

I had always believed that, and so I hadn't cared whether he treated me unkindly. And yet...

"I have decided that you are unworthy to be my fiancée. I will not allow you to get away with your outrageous schemes against Lainie!"

Lainie Cyan was the girl standing by Prince Algard's side. She was the daughter of the Baron Cyan, but until just recently, she had grown up as a commoner. Baron Cyan was similarly a former commoner, an up-and-coming aristocrat who had been permitted to join the ranks of the nobility in recognition of his many achievements.

Lovely was an excellent word to describe her. Her velvety hair was the color of the night sky; her downcast eyes had a certain appeal to them. She was less sophisticated than many of the other guests, but it was impossible to take your eyes off her. No one who saw her could possibly fail to take note of her. Given her beauty and origins, she had become the subject of considerable attention.

The reason I knew so much about her was because she had caught the attention of my fiancé, Prince Algard, too. Originally, our betrothal had been meant as a political alliance, at the request of the king. Perhaps that was why I had never felt any infatuation for my future husband. There was no denying that we had both allowed ourselves to go along with the arrangement out of a sense of duty and responsibility toward our country.

Perhaps that wasn't a good foundation for a relationship. Lady Cyan certainly possessed a certain charm that I lacked.

She had many genuine virtues—charm, the appeal of youth, and an earnestness that made one want to take her under their wing.

Even when rumors began circulating that Prince Algard was attending to her needs, I hadn't worried. I knew she'd had trouble adjusting to life at the academy, due to her humble origins. Perhaps, I thought, Prince Algard had been taking care of her for that reason. And that in and of itself was fine. How could I reproach him for coming to the aid of a fellow student?

And yet Prince Algard and I were still engaged to be wed, at least back then. That was why I had given her some candid advice about her excessive communication with a man who was soon to be married. That had been my only point of contact with her. Which was why I had no idea what Prince Algard meant when he said I had acted outrageously toward her.

"If you are referring to my exhortations toward Lady Cyan, I have no intention of harming her! Why on earth are you doing this *now*? And *here* of all places?!"

Rather, I felt as though *I* was the victim of Prince Algard's short temper. Our engagement had been decided by the state. It couldn't be overturned by the will of any single individual. And moreover, it was inappropriate of him to come out with something like this during a festive occasion. After all, the nobles who would one day become his vassals were here at this evening party, too.

I couldn't understand why he had acted this way, as he surely must have realized all this for himself.

"Prince Algard. If you don't mind me asking, has His Majesty approved of this?"

"I'll have him approve it later."

"Why do you want to call off a marriage arranged by your own parents?! Do you understand what you're doing?!"

"I won't allow my father to interfere, or my mother! I will decide my own path, by myself!" he snarled.

My breath caught, and I shook my head. I could hardly comprehend what he must have been thinking.

"But there are rules that must be upheld! Please, Prince Algard, think about what you're doing! When did you become so clueless?!"

"*I'm* clueless?! If anyone is clueless, it's you, Euphyllia! You're obsessed with your ambition to become queen! You aren't worthy!"

"I—I don't know what you're talking about…!"

I tried to muster my strength to explain myself, but Prince Algard was being utterly hostile toward me.

"Lainie has been subjected to bullying, the theft and damage of her personal belongings, and even an assassination attempt! I've been investigating these events, and what do I find? *You* were responsible for them all!"

I honestly didn't have the faintest knowledge of these accusations. I had never done anything of the sort. But before I could put in a word of defense—

"I can testify to her misdeeds. I've seen her plotting against Miss Lainie on a regular basis!" declared one of the young men standing behind Prince Algard.

I ground my teeth. "Navre Sprout, Moritz Chartreuse, and Saran Meckie…!"

These three were the sons of some of the most notable families in the country.

Navre Sprout was the son of the commander of the Royal Guard, responsible for protecting the capital. He had dark-green hair that looked black in lower light and sharp honey-colored eyes that were now narrowed and glaring my way.

Beside him was the nervous-looking Moritz Chartreuse, with his silvery hair and bewitching purple eyes. He was the son of the count presently presiding over the Ministry of the Arcane.

Slightly behind these two was Saran Meckie, so beautiful that his appearance alone could often prompt a sigh from unsuspecting onlookers. He wasn't a noble, but rather the son of an influential merchant family, and he had been enrolled at the academy as a special student.

I caught my breath. Each of these three individuals was particularly popular here at the academy. I stared back at them, almost biting my lips.

I knew they were Prince Algard's followers, and I had often seen them interacting with Miss Cyan. But only now did I realize they had framed me for tormenting her.

"Lainie may be a commoner, and her behavior at times may be a little unrefined, but Lady Euphyllia has gone too far with her abuse," Navre accused me in a strong, indignant tone of voice.

"Indeed, indeed. I always thought she was too cruel in her reprimands. And to think, she even had others do her bidding to avoid getting her own hands dirty!" Moritz added with an exaggerated wave of his arms. There was clear contempt in his eyes as he stared me down.

"Lainie has been trying so hard to fit in... She might not have your status, but we're all of the same flesh and blood." Saran shook his head in feigned disappointment.

I felt the stern gazes of those around me all turning my way. My breath caught for a moment, and then I protested. "I only ever offered Miss Cyan advice! I don't remember ever trying to harm her!"

"So arrogant, Lady Euphyllia! The daughter of our venerable duke, our honorable queen-to-be! You have forgotten yourself in your noble status!" Moritz shouted back harshly.

Murmurs of sympathy were rising inside the hall. I glanced around in disbelief.

"But I never instructed *anyone* to do anything to her! I've never once wanted to tear down Miss Cyan!"

"You're disgusting, Lady Euphyllia! Using others to bring a young lady to tears!" Navre bellowed.

But I had never given any instructions like that. I wanted to ask them who exactly had supposedly been involved in this plot, but I doubted my accusers would even deign to answer that question.

Why in the world was this happening? The suspicion and resentment were already spreading around me through the hall.

I tried to explain again that I hadn't done anything they were accusing me of. And yet my throat tensed, and I couldn't bring myself to speak. Only my lips quivered as I traced the words.

"I'm sorry, Euphyllia."

"Prince Algard…"

"Repent! Apologize to Lainie for what you've done, Euphyllia Magenta!"

What did I have to apologize for? I didn't understand any of this. I didn't even know what I had done wrong. I knew I had to plead my innocence, but my voice dried up, and I couldn't get a single word out.

I had suffered so much ridicule and scorn just to get to where I was today. For better or worse, my position as the fiancée of the next king had made me the subject of considerable attention. I had never thought of myself as weak. In fact, I always tried my best to stay strong. I had always done all I could to perfectly embody the expectations people had for me.

But was I…was I really *conducting myself the way everyone expected…?*

Once that shred of doubt had wormed into my mind, the strength bled from my knees. No one was listening to me. Nothing I said made any difference. I had always believed that if I simply behaved the way I thought was right, good things would naturally follow. But this wasn't at all what I had wanted.

This wasn't my first encounter with misfortune or disadvantages. This wasn't the first time I had been confronted by people trying to trip me up with malicious intent. But *these* people weren't malicious, from what I could tell—their actions seemed to be motivated by deeply held beliefs.

I couldn't understand that. That was why I was so shocked, why my knees were buckling, why I had been left wondering—*how could this happen?* I felt as if my legs were about to give way as reality sank in.

…That was when the air in the hall began to change ever so slightly.

"…Huh?"

I wasn't the only one who noticed it. Prince Algard glanced suspiciously toward the window from which the sound had emanated.

How should I describe it? It was like something was tearing through the air with great force—and screaming.

"AaaaaaaAAAAAAHHHH!"

It *was* screaming. And the next moment, something came smashing through the window.

"…Huh?"

I stood there petrified, all but forgetting I had been about to lose my strength. *Something* had come crashing through the window with such momentum that it rolled across the floor until it came to a stop between Prince Algard and me.

The tension in the air had been completely obliterated. Everyone in the room, including those who had dived out of the path of whatever had just joined us, was watching on in dumbfounded fascination.

"Ow… Lost control there. I guess I still need to do more research."

A beautiful girl stood up before us, brushing away the shards of glass sticking to her clothes with one hand.

She was wearing a jacket and trousers for ease of movement—attire that wasn't at all suitable for this social setting. And yet she positively emanated charm.

Her childish face was stained with soot, but her sense of grace remained unmarred. Or would it be more accurate to say her appeal came from that energy and vitality? I could only gaze at her, utterly captivated.

She picked up a device lying at her feet—broom-shaped but not quite a broom. Her eyes were a pale green, reminiscent of fresh verdure, although there was also a silly winsomeness about her.

And the color of her hair took everyone's breath away. It was platinum in color, just like Prince Algard's—proof of royal blood—and as she shook it, it struck me as even softer, even sunnier than his.

"You…!" Prince Algard's voice was trembling.

His expression had changed from one of astonishment to one of indignant rage.

In response, the girl who had become the center of all this commotion raised a hand in casual greeting. Then she spoke, her voice so cheerful that her earlier nervousness might as well never have been. "Ah, Allie…! Am I interrupting something?"

"S-Sister!" Prince Algard cried.

Princess Anisphia Wynn Palettia, the Kingdom of Palettia's famed *troublemaker*, flashed her younger brother a refreshing smile.

* * *

In the Kingdom of Palettia, there dwelled a certain princess.

She was the most powerful and troublesome girl in the history of the kingdom, its strangest and most eccentric denizen. She was the bane of the royal family and had earned herself a great many less-than-complimentary titles. Her name was Anisphia Wynn Palettia.

Her peculiarities and outlandish deeds seemed to grow exponentially by the day until none were surprised by whatever fresh disturbance she was responsible for.

It was said she could use the wind to carry herself into the sky and soar over the castle walls.

It was said she had burned herself all over while trying to heat up water for a bath.

It was said she had completely annihilated a monster that had been interfering with the construction of a new highway to the royal capital.

And it was said that her eccentricity had broken the king's heart when she declared she had no intention of marrying.

There were a great many anecdotes detailing Anisphia's strange deeds, so much so that if anything in the city seemed amiss, it was only a matter of time before it was discovered that she had some involvement in it.

She truly was the Princess Peculiar—a self-centered eccentric, part fool, part genius.

But people described her another way, too—as a genius who loved magic more than anyone, but whose love was unrequited.

Anisphia Wynn Palettia—a princess who lacked the gift of magic, a gift that came as a matter of course to every other member of the royal and noble ranks. And unable to use magic, she had become the heretical progenitor of the field of magical science, or as she called it, *magicology.*

* * *

Er, this could be a little awkward…

I—Anisphia Wynn Palettia—found myself standing before a group of well-dressed children, the sons and daughters of various noble families. I had just crashed a party, I was quite sure.

The stares being directed my way were uncanny. To be honest, I felt ill at ease. Had I just made another major blunder? It had been so long since my last one, too.

I had been conducting a nighttime test of my latest magical device, when I had thought it would be so lovely to reach up to the heavens to try to grab a star. That, however, had caused me to lose control and sent me crashing through a window. That mistake was going to get me in trouble, wasn't it…?

I checked my Witch's Broom, which helped me fly, for any damage. Luckily, it wasn't broken. I would have cried if it had been. At least it was only my reputation that had been injured! Everything was fine!

Glancing around again, I laid eyes on my younger brother, Allie! Hmm. I knew he didn't like me very much, so this interruption had probably left him utterly infuriated.

Huh? I've never seen her *before. Why is he hugging that girl so protectively?*

And everyone seemed to be sneering at the girl who was actually supposed to be engaged to him. Huh? What was going on here? Curious.

"Hey, Allie," I said. "Why are you holding that girl? Miss Euphyllia is by herself over there."

"…Th-this is none of your business!"

Ah, he was angry all right. I had expected as much, but he was glaring daggers at me. I mean, there was a lot of bad blood between us, but this struck me as something else.

It was all well and good for *me* to be a failure when it came to being a member of the royal family, but for him, our future king, to be standing beside someone other than his betrothed, our future queen consort? Unsure what to make of this, I turned my gaze to Miss Euphyllia.

"Er, Miss Euphyllia? What's going on? Is that girl going to be his concubine or something?"

Euphyllia was a daughter of the ducal Magenta family—and a particularly beautiful young lady. Her exquisite beauty had been the subject of admiration from many people.

Her hair was a pale silver in color, as though it had absorbed the light of the moon, and so delicate that I'm sure it would be soft to the touch. Her skin was fair and smooth, and her pink eyes made me think of roses. With her sky-blue dress, she stood out even amid everyone else at this flowery social gathering.

"Huh…?"

Turning my attention away from my brother, I called out to Miss Euphyllia, who seemed to be in a daze. All at once, her expression paled, and she averted her eyes.

"Huh? What's wrong?"

"No, it's just…"

Euphyllia, too? Her reaction was very unexpected. I had always seen her as someone unafraid of expressing her thoughts, even to adults—which was why I had often thought she would make such a good queen.

Nonetheless, it looked like she was on the verge of breaking down in tears. Had my sudden entrance through the window scared her that much?

…No, there had to be some other explanation. Noticing where she was standing, and the way everyone was hovering around her, an idea sparked in my memory. At that moment, it all came together for me. "…Ah, I see. So my brother started making false accusations and broke off your engagement?"

"—?!"

Euphyllia lifted her gaze, as if to ask how I could have possibly known. Her eyes were darting around in shock; her expression, normally as firm as an iron mask, was undergoing a marked transformation.

Huh. How about it? I remembered such stories from my *past life*, but to think that this sort of thing could actually happen! The world was a strange place. Although, I wasn't one to talk. Oh, the irony.

"Hmm, from what I can see, Miss Euphyllia does look rather friendless, no?"

"Er, um, how?"

"Hmmm… All right, that settles it!"

It wasn't good to bully a girl. I didn't know who was in the right here, but either way, it was time for some external arbitration. *Someone* needed to be Miss Euphyllia's champion, especially given that she had no other allies.

I had no idea what the situation was or who was in the wrong—but even if it turned out later that Miss Euphyllia *had* been at fault, I doubted anything bad would come to me from defending her now.

"Well, Miss Euphyllia? Let's go. I'm kidnapping you."

"…Huh?"

"I'm kidnapping Miss Euphyllia, so you can't hold her responsible for any of this! Come on, let's go now!"

"Huh…? Er…? Wh-what…?"

"So that's that, Allie! I'm taking her home with me! We can have a family discussion later!"

I approached Miss Euphyllia, who still looked taken aback, and threw her over my shoulder. *Heh. Sorry about this.*

In a real kidnapping, it would probably be best to take her in my arms, but at that moment, I wouldn't have been able to do anything if *both* my hands were occupied!

She let out a faint gasp as I pulled her up. My brother was also beginning to get impatient. Well, I wasn't about to stay here any longer to hear what he had to say!

"Wait, Sister—"

"See ya, Allie!"

Flashing my brother a grin, I began to run with Miss Euphyllia over my shoulder—then I leaped into the air, out through the window from which I had entered. Gravity would soon pull me back down to the ground.

Miss Euphyllia had a really good scream. "Wh—?! AAAAAHHHH-HHHHHH!"

"It's a no-rope bungee jump! Say hello to air travel, Miss Euphyllia!"

I grabbed the Witch's Broom and hooked my leg around it. At the same moment, I poured my magical energy into it—and so we began to gain altitude just before we could graze the ground.

Miss Euphyllia was still screaming, but it was time to go see my father!

* * *

In the Kingdom of Palettia, there lived a princess unloved by magic, ridiculed and despised for her inability to make use of the powers freely available to other members of the noble and royal ranks.

Nonetheless, this girl still adored magic, and so she took to constructing devices capable of re-creating, and even transcending, ordinary magic.

Thus began the first act of the journey of this legendary princess, whose feats (and eccentricities) would go on to leave an indelible mark on future history.

CHAPTER 1
The Reincarnated Princess
Can't Brake Suddenly

"…Hmm. That most certainly *was* a handful."

I unclenched my stiff shoulders. In front of me was a mountain of completed papers. Thankfully, my tension seemed to dissipate somewhat now that I had reached my goal for the day. Yet a king's work was never done, it seemed, no matter how much effort he puts into it.

"Excellent work as always, Your Majesty."

"Come now, Grantz. There's no need to be so formal."

The voice that had called out to me belonged to none other than Grantz Magenta, the head of the foremost house of the aristocracy, the ducal Magenta family, the chancellor of the realm of the Kingdom of Palettia, and above all, my close personal friend.

And the one to whom he had called was of course me, Orphans Il Palettia, the present sovereign of the Kingdom of Palettia. I had just completed my royal duties for the day.

"I could do with a cup of tea. Join me, Grantz."

"As you wish, Your Majesty."

"Again, so formal! Address me not as your king, but as your friend, now."

"…Very well, Orphans."

I nodded in satisfaction as his tone of voice relaxed.

Grantz might have been in his late thirties, but his youthful vigor had yet to show any sign of slowing.

I, on the other hand, looked older than my years, my hair graying noticeably. It was probably my constant fatigue to blame for that. I wasn't oblivious to the difference between us. We were so close in age, yet he was able to maintain his youth.

The Magenta family was graced with a long history. The dukes, having inherited royal blood, had also inherited the platinum hair of the royal family. Nonetheless, as the generations passed, that color had come to differ from my own. If anything, it was closer to silver now more than platinum.

But the most unique thing about Grantz was his eyes. Those reddish-brown irises were so intense and sharp that they seemed to contain scorching flames that could leave the faint of heart quaking in their boots with a glance. For better or worse, he had passed those eyes on to his daughter and son. The shared blood of the parent and child was difficult not to see.

"...The apple doesn't fall far from the tree, as they say," I murmured as I rang the bell to summon a maid to prepare a pot of tea.

Grantz must have heard my sigh, as he glanced across at me as he took a seat. "What's wrong? Are you worried about your children again?" he asked teasingly.

"How can I *not* worry?!" I replied in frustration.

I had a special fondness for Grantz's children, especially his daughter, Euphyllia, as though they were my own.

That was partly because she was engaged to my son, Algard—but more than that, it was my own rascal of a daughter who made me feel that way.

"She's been rather quiet lately, but I fear this is just the calm before the storm."

"Princess Anisphia *is* a bit of a storm herself, isn't she?"

"What are you laughing at? I've never once considered this a joking matter, Grantz."

There was a knock on the door, followed by the maid entering the room with a curtsy. She placed the pot of tea on the table nearby before leaving.

As I sipped at my cup, I let out another sigh. "She's already seventeen years old, and still there's no indication that she might settle down…"

"But if she were to *settle down*, as you say, she would hardly be Princess Anisphia anymore, no?"

"Stop it. I'm depressed enough as it is…"

"I'm afraid it can't be helped. After all, *we* were the ones who condoned her behavior in the first place back when it all began," Grantz responded, elegantly bringing his tea to his lips.

I curled my lip at that, but I had no argument for him. Perhaps it was stress again, but I could feel a heavy weight in my stomach. I let out resigned sigh.

"Why is there no end to problems requiring my attention?"

I'm sure anyone who saw me would have assumed I was in my fifties from my appearance. My platinum-colored hair, proof of my royal lineage, was conspicuously dull and gray.

Constant anxiety had carved deep furrows across my face, to the extent that seeing myself in the mirror was enough to sour my mood. That was proof that my responsibilities as king were a burden. But my biggest cause for concern was my daughter, mercilessly causing me trouble with no end in sight.

"But we *can* relieve those worries at least somewhat, wouldn't you say?"

"Hmm… Do you mean Algard and Euphyllia?"

"They will both be graduating soon. In the future, they will be asked to contribute as our future king and queen. And that will give them more opportunities to lead by themselves."

"…Assuming all goes well," I grumbled.

"…Are you concerned about that rumor?" Grantz asked back, narrowing his eyes.

I nodded by way of response. "Euphyllia will be fine, but that cursed Algard… It's all well and good for him to indulge himself with that baron's daughter, but he needs to learn to exercise moderation."

"It isn't easy gathering information from within the academy, but word has slipped out. It must be rather public by now."

Rumor had it that Algard was constantly spending time with the Cyan girl, while Euphyllia had been seen warning him to take care several times. The topic had become a subject of intense gossip among the nobility.

The Aristocratic Academy by its very nature was quite secretive, and so information from within its walls rarely reached the outside world. The fact that these rumors had leaked in spite of all that meant Algard must have been making a considerable scene. My stomach hurt just thinking about it.

"...Sorry, Grantz. It was the royal family who insisted on this engagement in the first place..."

"It's Euphyllia's duty to ensure that she doesn't lose her betrothed's heart. You are quite right that Algard needs to learn moderation, but this may serve as a wake-up call for the both of them."

Grantz's bluntness didn't mean he was unloving, loyal only to his official duties. Rather, his very affection for his daughter was why he had given her a strict education, so that she would have the strength to serve as the kingdom's next queen.

On the face of it, the Kingdom of Palettia was a paragon of peace. However, there were a great many problems buried under the surface. Years ago, when I started turning my thoughts to the future, I found myself fretting whether Algard would be able to support the country by himself, and so I had insisted he take Euphyllia, whose talents I had known since she was a child, as his fiancée.

Nonetheless, I couldn't help but notice a lack of love between them. Neither seemed to have any feelings for the other at all beyond duty, although that wasn't particularly unusual for a betrothal among two noble houses.

But this rumor had started circulating at a time when I was especially worried. I couldn't help but be concerned.

"But Euphyllia said she would take care of it, yes?"

"She did, and yet... I'm fully aware that the royal family wants this marriage to be a success, but if the entirety of the burden is placed on my daughter, we'll have no choice but to call off the engagement."

It wasn't easy to agree with that, but what Grantz had said was true. If that was what Euphyllia wanted, we would have no choice but to consider ending the betrothal plans. After all, it was the royal family, not her, who had initiated them, so it was up to us to clean up any mess they caused.

That was why I had gone so far as to ask Euphyllia whether she wanted to break off the engagement. But she had asked me to leave everything to her. In the end, I had presumed upon her generosity, but had she actually been able to find a resolution...?

I was stricken with an acute pang of anxiety, just as there came a sudden, vigorous knock on the door.

"Your Majesty! Urgent news!"

"What could possibly be urgent at this hour...? What's happened now?!"

"Princess Anisphia has visited the royal palace using a magical device! She's requesting an audience with you, Your Majesty!"

"What has that harebrained girl done now?!" I found myself exclaiming in a raspy voice.

Why couldn't she just behave herself for once...?!

"And also..."

"Also what?! Quit dawdling and come out with it!"

"Apologies! Princess Anisphia wants to see you, but she is accompanied by Lady Euphyllia Magenta... And we believe Her Highness may have kidnapped her!"

My eyes opened wide in alarm at this report, and my vision briefly went dark. I shook my head, trying to regain my composure, but I couldn't suppress the indignation welling up inside me.

"...Well then, what are you waiting for?! Bring her to me! Now!"

* * *

"Greetings, Father! I'm really sorry for dropping in like this!"

"Anis! What have you done this time?! And why is Euphyllia with you?!"

Whoa, my father was absolutely furious. Well, that wasn't an unreasonable response, all things considered.

I had abducted...ahem, *removed* Miss Euphyllia from that evening party at the Aristocratic Academy and taken her straight to the royal palace to request an audience with my father. She was still glancing around wide-eyed over my shoulder. Even the renowned perfect young noblewoman must have been terrified of the flight she had just endured.

"Please calm yourself, Your Majesty. Princess Anisphia, Your Highness, I do believe it has been a while."

"Oh? Duke Grantz is here, too? Well, that's convenient."

There was another figure in my father's office—Miss Euphyllia's father, Duke Grantz, my father's right-hand man. Convenient, indeed.

"...Euphyllia? How long are you planning to stay there?" Duke Grantz asked reproachfully.

"...Ugh...? F-F-Father?! E-excuse me! Princess Anisphia!"

Miss Euphyllia's face snapped up, and she rushed to get down from my back.

I released her hand, letting her kneel and bow her head.

"Ah, you don't have to do that...," I said. "Duke Grantz, please don't be too hard on her. She's probably a little shaken after everything that just happened."

"Anis! Explain yourself! What have you done this time? What are you doing with Euphyllia?" my father demanded.

"Well... I was out doing a nighttime test of my Witch's Broom, and the stars were so beautiful, so I kind of took my eyes off where I was going. And then I crashed into a party at the Aristocratic Academy!" I reported truthfully.

"...You fool of a girl!" my father cried out, rising to his feet and bringing his fist down on my head.

That strike was so painful it felt like stars were falling to the ground in front of my eyes. The back of my eyes grew warm, and I had to hold my head in my hands.

"That hurt, Father! You're awful!"

"I've had enough of your cheek! Why, you...you...you...!"

"I know it was wrong; you think I don't?!"

"If you're *really* sorry, don't do it again! How many mistakes do you have to make before you learn?!"

"Father, no one can make progress without making at least a few mistakes!"

"I'm telling you to take precautions! Repeating the same thing over and over is the height of folly, you imbecile! Is that head of yours just for show?!" he bellowed, bringing his fist down on my head a second time.

It was so painful that I had to crouch down, pressing my hands against my temples.

Ugh, his knuckles really hurt...! He was the worst! The absolute worst!

"...Ahem. Perhaps you've made your point? Princess Anisphia?" Duke Grantz called out to me, feigning a cough.

With that remark, my father came back to his senses and brought his seething anger under control. His complexion, however, was still rather pale.

The duke's sharp eyes were fixed on me. I couldn't help but feel a little ill at ease, but this was no different than usual, so I sat up straight and asked: "What can I do for you, Duke Grantz?"

"Why have you brought Euphyllia to the royal palace?"

"Ah, right, right! I came to deliver a report, Father!"

"And what would that be, Anis?"

"Allie said he was breaking off his engagement with Miss Euphyllia."

"...Huh?"

My father froze up, falling silent for a long, drawn-out moment. Beside him, Duke Grantz's eyes widened slightly, as though taken by surprise.

"I'm sorry, Anis. I'm a little tired, so I must have misheard. What was that again?"

"I said Allie was trying to break off his engagement with Miss Euphyllia."

"What?"

"He's breaking off the engagement."

"Whose?"

"His and Miss Euphyllia's."

I'd told him the facts multiple times, and my father stood there with his mouth hanging agape. I tried waving my hand in front of his eyes, but there was no reaction.

Finally coming back to his senses, my father rubbed his brow and asked in a shaky voice: "Algard...said that?"

"That's what I've been trying to tell you!"

"...I'm sorry. How I wish this was all a bad dream," he said in disbelief, before turning to Euphyllia. "Is it true?"

Euphyllia seemed to freeze up once again as my father took her in his sights, before she drooped her shoulders and lowered her head. "...Yes. I'm terribly sorry I wasn't able to keep everything under control."

With that, Miss Euphyllia bowed her head helplessly. She was so fragile that my hand found its way to her shoulder. My lips twitched as I sensed her trembling.

I could only imagine how she must have felt. To have her betrothed suddenly break off her engagement at an evening party... As dignified as she was, it was still no wonder that she was in shock.

"...What a mess! What on earth is that benighted son of mine doing?! Did he not think to ask me?! In the middle of a party no less?!"

"Please, Your Majesty, calm yourself."

"How can you possibly expect me to remain calm?!"

"Er, Father? I know you're angry, but Miss Euphyllia is in shock, so please don't yell..."

Now that I had pointed this out to him, my father lowered his voice, although he remained sour.

Duke Grantz let out a quiet sigh, before turning to his daughter. "...Euphyllia."

"I— I'm so sorry, Father... I'm useless, unworthy..."

Miss Euphyllia bowed her head even deeper, as though by now unable to raise it back up again. Her shaking was growing stronger by the second.

"I know I'm the one who brought it up," I interjected, "but Miss Euphyllia isn't feeling well, so can she sit down?"

"A-ah. Yes, of course..." My father nodded and helped guide her to a nearby set of sofas.

I sat beside my father, while Euphyllia and Duke Grantz took the seats across from us.

Once everyone had sat down and taken a few deep breaths, my father cleared his throat. The anguish on his face was obvious. Well, that wasn't much of a surprise, either.

"...I'm sorry I got so upset just now. But I can't believe it..."

"Well, it did happen, Father."

He held his head in his hands. I couldn't blame him. Allie and Miss Euphyllia's betrothal had meant they would be the future king and queen of Palettia. It was an incredibly important arrangement. That was why Miss Euphyllia, Duke Magenta's daughter, had been chosen as my brother's partner.

And that was why their engagement wasn't something that could be annulled so easily. Then again, Allie's announcement was so bizarre that it wasn't entirely surprising that our father had no idea how to respond.

"...Sorry, Grantz. I was overly optimistic. Naive, even," my father murmured, his head lowered, pressing a hand against his gut as though burdened with a stomachache.

Nonetheless, Duke Grantz quietly shook his head. "You shouldn't be so quick to apologize, Your Majesty...," he said, before turning to his daughter. "Euphyllia."

"...Yes."

"I've heard that your relationship with Prince Algard hasn't been progressing. It is most unfortunate that this has happened."

"...I'm terribly sorry."

"You don't need to apologize. What you need to think about now is how you will conduct yourself in the future."

"I'm willing to accept any punishment." Miss Euphyllia seemed to take her father's words to heart, awaiting his condemnation.

Duke Grantz's eyebrows twitched as he watched his daughter.

I had to interrupt the tense conversation between the two. "Ahem... Duke Grantz, if I may?"

"What is it, Princess Anisphia?"

"Forgive me for saying this, and I don't believe your intention is to blame Miss Euphyllia for what happened. However, I think the shock has affected her judgment. Could you be a little gentler with her? And you too, Miss Euphyllia. I know you must be startled by how sudden that was, but can you try to relax a little? Everyone here, myself included, is on your side."

Miss Euphyllia finally looked up with some confusion. She didn't have the faintest clue what I was talking about, did she?

I tried smiling back at her. "Anyway, let's straighten everything out first! Our fathers both seem to understand the situation, right?"

"...It doesn't feel right, hearing you say something sensible for once," my father remarked.

"How rude!"

"You can blame yourself for that!"

I didn't get it. Well, that was fine. I pursed my lips, when my father thanked me. "Anis. I'm going to put the matter of your trespass at the Aristocratic Academy aside for now. Even if it was all just a fortuitous coincidence, I want to thank you for looking out for Euphyllia."

"Well, it really was a coincidence."

"We have to go after Algard. If we can't convince him to show some self-restraint..."

"Ah, Father? I think some of his friends were involved, so you should make sure to deal with them, too."

He responded with disgust before reaching into his pocket and pulling out his favorite stomach medication, swallowing it down with a hint of melancholy in his eyes. That was probably partly because of the mess we were in, but I couldn't help but think he was tired of dealing with me, too. I was perfectly aware I had messed up here.

Still, I was technically an outsider to this matter. I might have been a member of the royal family, but I had renounced any right to succeed to the throne.

That was why I hadn't had any intention of getting involved in succession disputes, but thanks to a force majeure, or maybe an accident, it had been unavoidable this time. Well, we could talk about that later.

"It's important that we investigate what happened and how, but it's just as vital that we tidy this up. I'm talking about Miss Euphyllia's future."

"...Her future?" my father murmured, his voice filled with bitter regret.

At the moment, it didn't matter whether Allie had legitimately broken off his engagement. The problem was that he had brought outside attention to everyone involved by doing it in such a public place.

Now, the whole affair would make it rather difficult for Miss Euphyllia to get married in the future. An engagement broken off in public wasn't something that could easily be made right. And we couldn't ask Miss Euphyllia to get back together with Allie after such an experience.

So the next question concerned Miss Euphyllia's future. Being discarded by your fiancé would make you a huge joke at social gatherings. That would be even worse for the expected future queen. Furthermore, she was the daughter of the ducal family of Magenta, a distinguished house known for a great many noteworthy achievements.

Together, these factors would make her the perfect target for the scorn of her peers. If that happened, she could potentially have difficulty finding another marriage partner at all.

Once a young lady had been abandoned by a member of the royal family, the number of her potential suitors would become quite limited. This was a major problem—Miss Euphyllia's future was in grave jeopardy. Allie's actions were entirely one-sided here... Yes, this was bad from multiple standpoints.

"Given her talent, I wouldn't want to let her go too far—"

"You couldn't possibly marry her off to a foreign country!" I interrupted. "After all, she's your daughter! And a genius, too! A rare child prodigy, blessed by spirits! I've heard so many stories about her!"

Miss Euphyllia was by far the greatest young lady of her generation. She excelled not only in etiquette and propriety but in magic and martial arts, too.

And she was incredibly beautiful. Her silvery hair and snow-white skin perfectly complimented her dignified character. If I had to say anything negative about her, I might point to the sternness I saw in her eyes sometimes— but if she was going to be our next queen, that dignity of hers was generally a good thing.

That was why I had heard so many people say she was particularly suited to be our next king's bride. Even though I distanced myself from official matters, I had still heard of those rumors. To be frank, I felt she was far superior to me as a lady—not that I had ever bothered trying to be the perfect lady, mind you.

Maybe the respect I had for her was because we were both so different? Miss Euphyllia's talent had been evident from an early age, and so the royal family had pursued her as a bride for Allie. Her talents and abilities were widely regarded as immeasurable.

That was why it was out of the question to marry her off to another country—another land would have access to all her talents. If that happened, we would never see them again.

The issue now would be finding a partner more nearby. How many would be willing to marry someone who had once been betrothed to royalty, only to be cast aside for ostensibly stirring up trouble? On top of that, Miss Euphyllia belonged to a ducal family, so the pool of candidates of appropriate status was even narrower.

This was, in many ways, a dead-end situation. I glanced furtively her way; she was hunched over, carrying a dark shadow on her back.

No wonder. The expectation that she would one day become queen must have been an enormous burden throughout her upbringing. She had been raised to carry the whole kingdom in the future—and much more, too. *I* had fled that responsibility as fast as my feet could carry me.

To be honest, I had to admit that it might have been my abandonment of responsibility that led to this situation and her ruined future prospects.

Needless to say, her father was undoubtedly aware of how bleak the future now looked for her, too.

For that reason, Duke Grantz's continued silence was more than a little intimidating. But this wouldn't be a straightforward problem to solve—and any solution would need to be even more involved... Hmm. It would require a whole string of achievements.

At that moment, an idea suddenly popped into my head.

"Father!"

"What now?! There's no need to shout!"

"I've been thinking about Miss Euphyllia's future. Is it safe to assume that, given what's happened, you're worried about her marriage prospects?"

"...Yes, but what of it? Why do I have a bad feeling about this?"

"Then I have an idea!"

My father clearly didn't like the sound of this. So rude—it was almost as if he didn't think much of me!

Duke Grantz, still waiting in silence, turned his attention my way. The pressure of his stern gaze left me squirming in discomfort.

"What is this idea of yours, Princess Anisphia?"

"Yes. At present, Miss Euphyllia has been forced to break off her engagement and suffered a grave wound to her reputation as a noblewoman. Moreover, she's a person of rare talent. There's a high possibility you'll have to be very selective about her next suitor, and it's difficult to see what the future has in store."

"I suspected as much... So what is this idea of yours? I must say, I have a bad feeling about this," my father opined.

"Ha-ha, that's a bit rude. Even if you manage to get Allie to recant his one-sided declaration, the fact remains that Miss Euphyllia failed to stop him from coming out with it where he did."

Even if this was entirely Allie's fault, Miss Euphyllia hadn't been able to stop him from doing what he had done in public, which meant some would always doubt her suitability as his future bride. But now that it had happened, there was nothing that could be done about it.

"Essentially, Miss Euphyllia will also carry some responsibility in the eyes of others..."

"Indeed, that's true. She *is* at fault for not having discouraged Prince Algard sufficiently."

"And that may not go away, but it's possible to recover from it. I think it would be good if we could give her a chance to do just that."

Duke Grantz kept his gaze locked on me this whole time, as though not to miss a single word.

In the midst of this strange tension, my father seemed both flustered and confused. "So...what are you trying to say? Out with it!"

"I'll get straight to the point, then... Father, Duke Grantz! Please give Miss Euphyllia to me!"

If I had to describe in one word the atmosphere that descended on the room then, I would say that it *froze*. My father's face twitched, while Duke Grantz's eyes widened ever so slightly.

And Miss Euphyllia, the person at the center of all this, raised her head, staring straight at me.

I flashed her a smile, before turning back to my father and Duke Grantz: "I'll do everything I can to make her happy! Please give us your approval!"

"Wait, wait, wait, wait, wait! What delusional nonsense are you blabbering about now?!" My father jumped to his feet, pale with fury.

Delusional?! I was being perfectly serious here!

"Princess Anisphia. You're asking me to *give* you my daughter? What exactly are your intentions?" Duke Grantz asked me, his tone returning to normal.

I nodded. "I would like to invite Miss Euphyllia to be my assistant."

"...Your assistant?" Miss Euphyllia was tilting her head to one side in confusion.

Her mannerisms were so cute that I wanted to pet her.

Perhaps having sensed my feelings, my father's gaze sharpened.

I cleared my throat, trying to regain my composure. "You must already know that I'm a proponent of magicology, but I would like Miss Euphyllia to assist me in my research and to help present it to the public."

"...Do I understand you correctly, Princess Anisphia? Do you mean to have my daughter take credit for your magicology achievements?"

"Yes! That's exactly it, Duke Grantz!"

Magical science, or *magicology* for short, was the name I had given to my research and my attempts to re-create the fantastical sights I had glimpsed in my past life—and to use those ideas to solve the mysteries of magic. My Witch's Broom had been one such idea, an invention born from my desire to harness the power of magic to achieve manned flight.

"With my father's approval, I've been able to spread some of my magicology ideas, albeit on a very small scale. But given my personal circumstances, I've refrained from publicly announcing my major accomplishments."

"Magicology was born from a revolutionary idea. And your magical tools were in turn born from magicology. You're afraid that the repercussions for the Kingdom of Palettia would be too immense...no?"

"Yes. So I promised Father I wouldn't make waves with the fruits of my research. The next king of Palettia may have some trouble if his elder sister was seen to shine too brightly."

While Allie might have been my younger brother, being a male, he had priority in the line of succession to the throne. That said, I previously had a claim as a member of the royal family—emphasis there on the past tense.

You see, I couldn't use magic. I was a princess, and yet I couldn't use magic, so in spite of all my magicology achievements, I couldn't be accepted as queen because of the way this country was run.

To put it simply, the Kingdom of Palettia had developed hand in hand with magic throughout its history. The First King had made a pact with spirits and founded the realm using the magical gifts they had granted him.

Next, the nobility had joined the king as his vassals, and so the

Kingdom of Palettia was established. That was why being able to use magic was essential for members of the royal family—yet I was unable to do so.

My inability to use magic had been disconcerting for everyone. And so I decided that if I was unable to use magic myself, I would study a new kind of magic that I *could* use. That was why I had abandoned my claim to the throne, so I could instead pursue my research. After all, I had thought that trying to juggle the two would only introduce unnecessary conflict.

My father had resisted at first, but I had been so insistent that he had resigned himself to my will. And so I became a princess in name only, not involved in political affairs, although still recognized as a member of the royal family.

"That being said, my father has been giving me a lot of work lately, and I think I'm getting to be kind of famous."

"Oh, that is rich! It's the other way around! I determined that, after your conspicuous escapades, I had better try to keep you occupied with something sensible, you unthinking, fool girl!"

"Huh...?"

Wasn't it rather dishonest of him to try to impose political troubles on me for such a selfish reason?

I usually didn't like to complain, because it tied directly into my hobby, but... Ah, I got sidetracked there. I had better get back to the matter at hand, I realized.

"I want to spread magicology, but I don't want to take center stage. So I thought, why not make my research a joint effort and let Miss Euphyllia take the credit?"

"...Indeed. That may well be enough to overshadow the annulment of her betrothal."

"You see? Oh, and there's one other thing. I can't use magic, so I need an assistant who can—and I can't think of anyone better than Miss Euphyllia!"

"...Really?"

"Yes! You're a talented noblewoman, a martial artist, beloved by spirits, and said to have the highest aptitude for magic of anyone in all of history! It's no exaggeration to say you're one of the Kingdom of Palettia's greatest treasures!"

In this world, magic was considered a gift from the spirits. And Miss Euphyllia was renowned for her ability to effectively employ a wide range of magic.

To be honest, I wished I had her talents—my envy was so strong I could almost taste it. Being the way that I was, the results of my research wouldn't be positively received by the rest of the nobility.

My deficiencies also meant I couldn't hire an assistant through the usual channels, no matter how much I wanted one. So Miss Euphyllia was perfect! It sounded a bit wrong to say that this was all thanks to her failed engagement, but that was no reason to let the opportunity go to waste. In the end, this would be to her benefit, too!

"...It certainly does make sense. I have to agree with you there," Duke Grantz remarked.

"You see?! So what do you think, Father? Will you approve?"

"Anis... Do you remember what you told me when you renounced your claim to the throne?" My father crossed his arms, his expression muted.

What was *that* supposed to mean? But I immediately hit on the answer and slammed my fist against my palm.

"...Ah, you mean that declaration of hers?" Duke Grantz must have known about it, too, because for whatever reason, he let out a weak sigh.

Miss Euphyllia's gaze wandered back and forth between the two men in confusion. "Father. Um... What are you talking about?"

"...When Princess Anisphia first broached renouncing her claim to the throne, she said, 'I don't want to marry a man. If I'm going to love anyone, I want to love a woman.'"

At Duke Grantz's words, Miss Euphyllia stared across at me, her eyes open wide.

Her gaze felt a little distant... But it was true. I had been completely serious.

"I mean, I don't want to get married and have children."

"You fool girl, yooooouuuuu!" my father cried out, grabbing me in a claw hold.

"Aaagh! That hurts! That hurts, Father! Let me go, please!"

My father grabbed me, screaming as his fingers dug into my face. The next thing I knew, he had lifted me up so my feet weren't even touching the ground! *Stop—it really hurts!*

"You treat your royal station and your responsibilities like rubbish under your feet...!"

"Ow! B-but...! But if you let *me* inherit the throne... I mean, I can't even use magic...! You've got your priorities backward...! I— I'm not wrong!"

"You're beyond wrong, you fool girl! Your magicology has value, I'll grant you that, but what makes you think you can never get married?!"

"You gave me your word! You said if I can produce results, I wouldn't have to! Ever! Owwwww! Father, look at your face! I can't even recognize you...!"

"It's a million times better than the pain in the gut you gave me back then!"

Finally, my father released me—well, more like threw me. Damn, that hurt. I had thought he was going to crush me there.

It was certainly true that, when I had made that declaration, I had faced a hellscape of screaming and shouting, and I did feel some regret in hindsight. But I meant what I said, so it would have inevitably come out sooner or later. In effect, all I did was nip it in the bud according to my own timing.

Because of that, there were all kinds of rumors about me—namely that I was attracted to girls.

I wasn't about to deny it. I *did* like girls! I had nothing against men, but when it came to topics like romance, engagement, or marriage, I just couldn't see myself in that picture.

"...Princess Anisphia. May I ask you a question?"

"Duke Grantz? What is it?"

"Do you mean that you *only* want Euphyllia as your assistant?" The duke fixed me in his sights, his unyielding gaze peering into my very mind.

"Hmm. It's true that her noble status and abilities with magic will be a boon, but to be honest with you…"

"…Yes?"

"Miss Euphyllia is just the kind of girl I like!"

"Are you capable of holding your tongue for a single moment, Anis?!"

"No!"

"You're making me angry again…!"

This time, I ran behind the sofa that Duke Grantz was sitting on so my father couldn't grab my face again. At that moment, my gaze met with Miss Euphyllia's perfectly, and she pulled back slightly.

That came as a small shock. Well, maybe that was unavoidable? I mean, I hadn't denied the rumors. But if I was going to recruit her, this could be a problem.

"Ah, um? If you don't feel the same way, I won't come after you. And I'm not a philanderer, either, so you don't need to worry about that. There are plenty of reasons why I want to get along with Miss Euphyllia."

"…With *me*?"

"I mean, I've never even been able to invite you to tea, seeing as you're Allie's fiancée and all! The situation isn't good, honestly, but I welcome it! You must think it was a disaster, too, right? So why don't you come and study magicology with me?"

"…Because these circumstances are *convenient* for you?" The corners of Miss Euphyllia's lips rose almost self-deprecatingly, and she averted her gaze.

Of course, I could understand that she was depressed at the sudden end to her engagement.

"That's true, but there's more to it."

"…?"

"You're free to join me for whatever reason you like, Miss Euphyllia. You're hurting, and I want to help you. You can take those words at face value, or you can believe me for any other reason. I don't mind."

Miss Euphyllia's eyes widened. I reached out and gently touched her cheek, then turned her head toward me. Up close, I could say with great certainty that her beauty was the real thing.

Whenever I had laid eyes on her from a distance, she had always been wearing a picture-perfect smile or no expression at all. But now she was unable to hide her true emotions, her eyes glistening with confusion and anxiety.

"If you don't believe me, I'll stop trying to recruit you. If that's what you want, I won't stop you. But if you change your mind someday, if you want me to help you then, that will be enough for me." I stroked Miss Euphyllia's head, hoping to ease the burden and pain that had been forced on her. "You can change your mind later if you want. So I hope you'll join me for your own reasons. Reasons you've chosen."

Miss Euphyllia stared back at me in a daze, like a lost child who didn't know what to do.

"Euphyllia?" said Duke Grantz, catching his daughter's gaze. The two of them were sitting on the same sofa, but he was on her other side. Her face was like a blank theater mask. He exhaled slowly. "...I'm sorry."

My eyebrows rose in astonishment at the duke's sudden apology, as did my father's.

Yet it was Miss Euphyllia who had the most notable reaction. She stared up at him with an expression of disbelief. "Father?"

"Euphyllia. As our expected next queen, you have made every effort not to bring shame to the Magenta family. But I suppose it was *I* who asked this of you in the first place." Slowly, as though choosing his words with great care, Duke Grantz began to convey his thoughts.

At that moment, he struck me as more of a clumsy father than a noble duke. His usual shrewdness was nowhere to be seen as he continued with palpable regret. "I thought that if you were responding to my wishes, it was right to nudge you along. As a strict father, I thought it only appropriate to treat you as the future bearer of the Magenta name."

"...What—what are you saying?!"

"I... I feel as though I may have made a grave mistake."

Miss Euphyllia leaned forward, shaking her head in disbelief. There was a hint of apprehension in her eyes—even fear. "It's thanks to your education that I'm the person I am today! I treasure it! I have no regrets! And you certainly weren't in the wrong, Father! It's all my fault! I'm just a fool, unworthy to be a duchess or a queen. I have dragged the name of my house through the mud!"

"My daughter is no fool," the duke interjected.

His firm denial cut off Miss Euphyllia's heartbreaking tears with a single stroke. They had taken *me* aback, but more importantly, Miss Euphyllia visibly jumped in surprise, her body trembling at the force of her father's assertion. Her mouth opened and closed in silence, as if she wanted to say something but couldn't quite put it into words.

Duke Grantz, staring straight at his speechless daughter, continued. "You have more than lived up to my expectations... Now I wonder whether I might not have smothered your own ambitions. If so, I am to blame."

Given Duke Grantz's usual dignity, this was unimaginable. It was hard to imagine that such an eminent member of the kingdom's nobility had actually just admitted this. And yet those words were his true feelings.

But Miss Euphyllia couldn't accept them so easily. "What are you saying...?" Her voice rose with grief. "Please stop, Father. Don't say any more, please. I won't know what to do with myself if you go on!"

"Indeed. One can't know. When you are faced with such trials, you can ask for help."

Duke Grantz's expression faltered. It was a slight change, but his forced smile was enough to betray his consternation. He reached out his hand and stroked his daughter's head.

Miss Euphyllia stared back at him, unbelieving.

"You're still a child, Euphie." The duke continued to stroke her head with an unaccustomed yet unquestionably caring hand. They were almost like any common parent and child. "I've stopped your heart from growing. I never taught you to grieve when you feel sorrow, to hurt when you're in pain. And now you're practically an adult. I kept on acting like you were the same little Euphie. All I taught you was how to put up a convincing front."

Miss Euphyllia's face visibly distorted in response to her father's words, becoming an indescribable expression that seemed both tearful and full of poorly hidden anger.

"Please stop, Father. Don't disparage yourself for my sake…! If anyone should be reproached, it's *me*! *I'm* the one who failed!"

Miss Euphyllia's pained cry was a testament to her love for her father as she insisted she alone was in the wrong.

Yet her father's smile only deepened in response to her appeals. "If you failed, then so did I—as a parent and as a man. I had high hopes for you, as the future leader of this country. But at the same time, I was too strict. I disciplined myself to dismiss your suffering, to ignore the hardships that lay ahead. I clothed you with armor, but I failed to strengthen the body inside. I'm ashamed."

"Father…!"

Miss Euphyllia shook her head in denial, sending tears spilling down her cheeks as she brushed off her father's hand.

Duke Grantz moved to wipe away her tears anyway; it was a truly fragile sight.

"I forgive you. Even if the king himself desires this engagement to proceed, I'll help you to decline it if that is what you want."

"…!"

"So tell me, Euphie, if you don't want to be queen…"

Miss Euphyllia bristled, biting down on her lip. But before she could draw blood, she slowly relaxed, as though the threads supporting her had finally broken. She covered her face in her hands. "…I'm sorry, Father. I can't do this anymore…"

Her breath was ragged, her words broken and barely audible. She sounded as though she might start crying again.

Duke Grantz nodded in silence. "I see…Very well. Thank you for telling me."

"…Yes. I should have relied on you more for support, Father. I thought

I had to be independent if I was to be the next queen. I couldn't rely on my parents..."

"That's good to keep in mind, Euphie. But sometimes, a wise noble needs to know when to call on the people around them."

"...Yes." Miss Euphyllia gave him a short nod.

The duke seemed relieved. He placed a hand on his daughter's shoulder before continuing. "Euphie. I think you should let Princess Anisphia take you under her wing. But the choice is yours."

"Huh...?"

"You will undoubtedly face a great deal of scrutiny after what's happened. It isn't hard to imagine how that might turn out."

As it was now, there would almost certainly be a commotion if Miss Euphyllia were to appear in public. At best, she would be the subject of questioning; at worst, of slander. This was a huge scandal, and the best option was to lie low.

"...So why should I join Princess Anisphia?" Miss Euphyllia asked, her face weary.

Duke Grantz pressed his lips together. He glanced my way for a second before continuing, "You're probably aware that Princess Anisphia lives in a villa on the grounds of the royal palace. It's much less conspicuous than the main residence. Most of all, it's located within the palace confines. If something were to happen, I would be able to come to your aid at once, and it should serve as a suitable retreat. Then, of course, there is also the princess's proposal. I don't think it's such a bad idea."

"Father..."

"You've worked hard and done your best. You need time to be not the daughter of a duke or future queen, but to be yourself. Princess Anisphia isn't looking for your title here."

"Well, I guess that's true..."

I wanted Miss Euphyllia because of her personal qualities. Duke Grantz must have heard me muttering to myself, as he nodded for her.

Right now, he was a father who only wanted what was best for his daughter.

"Take some time to think about what you want to do with your life, Euphie."

"But won't that cause issues for the family...?"

"I won't let something like this affect me or our family. Will you trust me?" asked Duke Grantz, returning to his usual aristocratic countenance.

Miss Euphyllia held her breath for a second before letting it out and nodding. "...Of course I do."

"In that case, what you do next depends on your own feelings... It would be wrong for me to ask to you to decide here and now."

Turning away from his daughter, the duke leveled his gaze at me. "In any event, we're going to have to get to the bottom of this. In the meantime, I don't want any unnecessary interference. So, Princess Anisphia, would you look after my daughter for a while? Euphie, you can spend this time thinking about whether to accept her offer."

"Of course! I'd be more than happy to!" I replied, filled with so much joy that I leaped into the air. Huzzah!

My father, on the other hand, seemed to have another headache. "...Anis. Please don't do anything reckless."

"You really are rude, Father!" I protested.

"Not as rude as you!" he murmured, drooping his shoulders in exhaustion.

Why did he have to act this way?

Miss Euphyllia wasn't about to reject her father's advice, but she was staring at me somewhat anxiously.

I smiled back at her, holding out my hand. "We might only have a short time together, Miss Euphyllia, but I'm pleased to have you."

"...Yes, Princess Anisphia."

"Just call me Anis. And can I call you Euphie?"

"Huh? I—I don't mind..."

"Yay! Nice to meet you, Euphie!"

I shook her hand up and down, beaming with joy. Euphie let out a chuckle, too, though her eyes seemed somewhat bewildered.

I hoped that one day I would see her smile for real, from the bottom of her heart.

* * *

"...Are you sure about this, Grantz?" I asked, shortly after Anis and Euphyllia took their leave.

Grantz remained silent for a moment, staring at the door. "It's for the best. After the annulment of her engagement, Euphie won't be able to appear in public for a while."

"Do you really think *this* is for the best? My Anis? Are you really sure about this?"

"Is your daughter so unreliable?"

Yes, I almost said, before clamping my mouth shut. In fact, Anis's novel ideas were often a great help to me, too. In spite of her unconventional approach, in spite of her flaws, she *did* have her redeeming qualities. Given her usual behavior, however, I wasn't comfortable admitting that.

I noticed the tension in my forehead and tried to relax, letting out a deep sigh as I rubbed my eyebrows.

"This is a good precaution, too, in the unlikely event that someone tries to attack Euphie."

"Grantz?!"

"It's a possibility. So it makes sense to have her stay close to Princess Anisphia."

"What are you saying?"

For a moment, I stared back in alarm, unable to even gauge what he was hinting at.

Grantz stared back at me, our gazes meeting. "Depending on what happens next, Prince Algard may have to step down."

"...Surely not?" I murmured.

It wasn't difficult to imagine what my friend was thinking. But it seemed like such an outlandish suggestion that I had to deny it.

Despite my astonishment, Grantz's gaze remained as firm as ever, his eyes glinting with a determined light. His resolution was firm.

"I will take action myself if necessary, Orphans. Even if Princess Anisphia refuses," he declared clearly.

Finally able to respond, I gave him a bitter grimace.

If what he was imagining did come to pass, just how would my rascal daughter react? It was easy enough to envision.

"...She'll cry. And resist."

"That's why we should begin to lure her now. To slide the collar around her neck, so to speak."

"Treat her like a beast, you mean?"

"Or a creature of legend, perhaps."

"What's the difference?"

She was still a princess, but I had to agree with Grantz.

After some more stiff discussion with my good friend, I finally relaxed. This was a troublesome matter that had been brought to my attention, and I couldn't afford to leave it unresolved. Depending on the outcome, Grantz's expectations for the future could well become reality.

It wasn't difficult to imagine Anis accepting such a turn of events. Changing the order of succession, forcing her brother to step down—what would that mean for her? Just thinking about it darkened my mood once again.

Grantz must have been able to guess what I was thinking. Nonetheless, he seemed amused.

"It would be a sight to see, though—Princess Anisphia ruling as queen regnant."

CHAPTER 2

The Reincarnated Princess
Makes a House Call

After the meeting with my father and Duke Grantz, I found myself walking through the corridors of the royal palace with Euphie by my side. In the end, everyone had decided it would be best for her to stay with me for a while.

There was a spare room in the villa that served as my residence, and so Euphie would stay with me there.

As for the villa I called my home, it was officially known as a detached palace, but my father had originally built it to isolate me. That being said, it was designed to *be* a palace, and there were plenty of rooms for people to live in. It would be used as a regular secondary palace after I was gone, in all likelihood.

But that also meant it wasn't difficult to prepare a room for one guest, and it was decided that Euphie's necessities and belongings would be brought after we had a chance to officially visit Duke Magenta.

Though we were walking side by side, Euphie said nothing as we made our way down the corridor. She remained one step behind me, leaving me feeling somewhat uncomfortable.

"Hey, Euphie. You'll be staying with me at my villa starting today, but is there anything you want to know?"

"No, not really. If there are any rules, I'm happy to follow them…"

"There are no rules, really. Only my personal maid and I live here. We're free to do whatever we want, more or less."

"Ah…"

Hmm. That was a somewhat indifferent response. Was she nervous? Or maybe she had always been a woman of few words?

Seeing as she had been my brother's fiancée, I had of course noticed her from a distance, and we had exchanged brief greetings on a few occasions, but this was my first time properly speaking to her. Plus, what with how unreceptive she was acting, I wasn't quite sure what to say next.

I knew I shouldn't be acting so cheerful after her traumatic end to her engagement. But I couldn't afford to leave her, either. Which meant we would have to do this the hard way!

"All right! Let's go to the detached palace! At times like this, you need a change of pace!"

"Huh?"

Though she seemed taken aback, I quickly embraced her in a hug, swept her up into my arms, and took off as fast as I could run.

"H-huh?! Lady Anis?! Why are you carrying me?! P-please put me down!"

"It's fine! Come on! You know what they say, right? Good deeds should be done quickly!"

"I—I can walk by myself! A-and besides, what if people…?!"

Don't worry about that! I ignored her protests, dashing through the corridors of the royal palace.

She tried to resist at first but quickly grabbed ahold of my clothes while I was running.

"H-how can you run through the corridors carrying someone in your arms…?! This truly is most unheard of!"

"Ha-ha-ha! You should have told me earlier!"

We sped past knights and maidservants in the employ of the royal palace, but they merely smiled back at me and pretended not to have seen us. It was always like this!

Euphie was blushing slightly, curling up in my arms as though to shield her face. That made her easier to carry, so I said nothing.

I sped onward as though to shake off the stares falling on me. Finally, we arrived at my villa on the outskirts of the palace grounds, and I set Euphie down once we reached the entrance.

The second she was free, she hurried to distance herself from me.

"This is my home, Euphie."

"...I'm aware of that." She nodded, letting out a sigh.

I watched her reaction as I reached for the door, only for it to swing open before I could even touch the handle. The person on the other side was a woman in a maidservant's uniform. Her reddish-brown hair was tied up in a bun, her blue eyes concealing all emotion.

"I'm back! Ilia?"

"Welcome home, Princess," Ilia said softly after giving me a small bow.

Ilia had been my exclusive maid for many years now, and the lack of warmth was business as usual for her.

"Your Highness. May I ask you a question?" she asked.

"What is it, Ilia?"

"Why is Prince Algard's fiancée, Lady Euphyllia, with you?"

"Because she's staying with us for the foreseeable future!"

"I see. I must admit I don't quite follow, but shall I prepare a room for her?" Ilia murmured, relaxing her shoulders.

Euphie observed our conversation as if it were some strange spectacle. I wanted to tell her that this was just how Ilia always was.

"Hmm. It's late, so how about you stay in my room tonight? Euphie?"

"...Huh? L-Lady Anis?!"

"No, no! I don't mean in an improper way!"

"But it *is* still improper...!"

"Ilia! Could you make us some tea?" I called out.

"Very well," Ilia responded, showing us to the next room.

Euphie looked like she still wanted to say something, but she followed my lead and entered. We made our way straight to the sitting room, which was set aside to welcome guests, and sat down to wait for the pot of tea.

"Please take a seat, Lady Euphyllia," Ilia prompted.

"...Thank you."

Euphie sat herself down on one of the sofas, a magnificent piece of furniture characteristic of the royal palace. I took a seat across from her while Ilia began to prepare the tea.

As she set about her preparations, Euphie watched in interest. My guest probably wasn't familiar with these Thermal Pots that we used here.

My Thermal Pot was a magical device designed to be placed atop a specially crafted base and served to keep water at a suitable temperature for tea, so it could be prepared instantly.

"...Is this hot water? But there's no fire. How does that pedestal work?"

"It's a magical device that uses a fire stone to keep the water warm. It's set to maintain a constant temperature, so there's hot water ready whenever you feel like a cup of tea or whatnot."

With this, there was no need to boil fresh water each and every time. Using this system, the detached palace was designed so hot water could be accessed through taps and faucets, just like in my past life.

"It's a bit of a hassle to set the temperature, though," I explained. "But once you've got it calibrated, you can use it over and over so long as you have a fire stone. It's good for more than just tea, too. We use them to warm up baths, for example."

"And thanks to this, I don't have to dip my hands in cold water when I wash the dishes," Ilia added.

"I see..." Euphie nodded in admiration.

I swelled with pride. My Thermal Pot was another successful result of my magicology research as I attempted to re-create my memories of conveniences from my past life.

My father enjoyed using some of the magical tools I had invented during the course of my research, too. The Thermal Pot was one of his favorites, and he used one to boil water and brew tea for himself whenever he was working late or didn't want to trouble one of the maids.

"Here you go, Lady Euphyllia."

"Thank you."

Euphie sipped at the cup of tea Ilia had hastily prepared for her and let out a sigh of relief. Once my cup was ready, I took a drink, too. Delightful.

"This Thermal Pot does appear very convenient," she remarked. "I can imagine quite a few other uses for it, too."

"Indeed," I responded. "We're using them all throughout the detached palace here."

"It certainly *is* convenient," Ilia added. "A little *too* convenient, or so I think at times."

"Oh? How so?" Euphie tilted her head to one side in puzzlement.

"I'm sure I don't have to explain that tools like this are unavailable outside the palace. If you get too used to the comforts we have here, you may miss them dearly once you go somewhere else."

"You're my personal maid, Ilia, so you don't have to worry about anything like that."

"Yes, I can't hope to be reassigned to another job. I'm trapped here."

Ilia pretended to cry, yet her expression remained uncannily vacant. If she was going to playact, she could at least make it a little more convincing...

"I'm glad to have had you taking care of me all these years, you know, Ilia?"

"That's quite a thing to say, given you're the one who ensured I could never escape."

"Ha-ha-ha! What a terrible thing to do, right?!"

"Yes, indeed. I'm still amazed that such a devilish person walks among the rest of us humans."

"I *am* human, Ilia. Do you need your eyes examined?"

This kind of back-and-forth always happened with Ilia. And *she* was the one who benefitted most from my magical devices.

It was thanks to our long years together that we could engage in this friendly banter. She had always been one of my favorite women, and I felt comfortable talking to her since I was a child and she a maid working at the royal palace. Perhaps that was why my father had asked her to be my chaperone.

We had been through a lot since then, and now we could exchange all manner of light conversation, peppered with a little irreverence here and there. Her attitude was exactly what I wanted, too. I wasn't fond of stiff formalities, and I knew she really was a nice person at heart. That being said, it was only natural that others considered us strange.

Such as Euphie, who was watching us in shock. It was little wonder.

Even if Ilia was my personal maid, it must have seemed quite out of the ordinary for her to speak so frankly with someone of such a vastly different social status.

"So, Princess. What *is* Prince Algard's fiancée doing here?"

"Well, Allie basically broke of their engagement in public, so I kidnapped her for her own protection."

"…I still don't follow. What were *you* doing there? Why would Prince Algard break off his engagement in public? If that's meant to be a joke, I fail to see the humor." Ilia's expression was quizzical as she came out with more questions.

Her reaction wasn't at all an unreasonable one, though. Euphie was the daughter of Duke Magenta, the kingdom's anticipated future queen, and so the expectations people had for her were immense. And in spite of all that, her fiancé had called everything off. It must have given my father quite the headache.

"I'm afraid it's the truth. Reality often unfolds in ways beyond our wildest imagination, don't you think?"

"I see. Of course, your imagination is especially wild, so I wonder if anyone would be convinced of that?"

"How rude!"

Disrespectful though that comment was, this was how Ilia and I normally interacted. Our conversations were practically banter. Meanwhile, Euphie seemed to shrink the friendlier Ilia and I were with each other.

Realizing that she seemed uncomfortable, Ilia cleared her throat. "And? So why did you bring Lady Euphyllia *here*, exactly?"

"I hatched a plan to hire her as my assistant! That way, we can offset any damage to her reputation from the engagement fiasco!"

"…Are you being serious?" Ilia stared at me with eyes as expressionless as those of a dead fish.

I nodded back at her.

With that, Ilia turned her gaze to the forlorn girl sitting with us. It was as though she were staring at a cow about to be shipped off to the hinterlands.

Euphie seemed quite bewildered by that stare.

Ilia released a sigh and turned back to me with visible sympathy and disdain. "You've finally lost your mind. I'm very sorry, Your Highness. I always knew you had a penchant for unknowingly bringing misfortune down on those around you, but I never suspected you would purposefully try to drive others to ruin."

"Huh...? But it's the other way around!"

"Ah, so you *do* mean well. But the road to hell is paved with good intentions, you know? Lady Euphyllia, please allow me to express my deepest condolences..." With that, Ilia bowed her head, truly remorseful.

Euphie could only glance back and forth between Ilia and me in consternation.

"Ilia?" I said, my lips twitching. "You really *are* terrible, you know that?"

"Ah... Are you sure, Your Highness? I know for a fact that *I* will never be able to escape this place, so I know more than anyone what this will mean for Lady Euphyllia. I speak only from experience."

Her attitude, her tone of voice, the way her shoulders wilted—it was as though I was a child who wouldn't listen.

Ilia cleared her throat before continuing. "Have you finally gone mad, Your Highness? No, you've been this way since the beginning. I feel very sorry for you."

"It's your own remarks you should feel sorry about!" I protested. "Why do you think so little of me?!"

Despite my complaints, Ilia turned away in disinterest. Truly, she had tremendous nerve. But then again, that was why I liked her so much.

The next moment, Ilia turned her gaze devilishly toward Euphie. "Lady Euphyllia, please don't be too hasty."

"E-excuse me?"

"Don't let this devil seduce you with her sweet words. Do you understand what I'm saying? Once you take her hand, it will all be over. She'll drag your soul down into the abyss, and there will be no coming back."

"Wh-what...?"

"Ilia, your perception of me seems a bit low. Can we discuss this later?"

I fixed her with a cold glare, but Ilia expressed nothing but heartfelt disappointment. I just couldn't decipher her.

"...Is she really so dangerous?" Euphie asked, glancing furtively—and doubtfully—my way.

No, my reputation was in freefall!

Ilia let out a deep sigh and pinched the bridge of her nose. "In the end, yes. But there are quite a few complications."

"So you don't recommend I stay?"

"Well. If it's what you truly want, Lady Euphyllia, and so long as you understand the risks, I have nothing more to say. On the other hand, can I assume that *she* didn't explain everything to you?" Ilia said, motioning toward me.

I averted my gaze. I—I didn't mean to leave anything out, you know?

"...No, it's just, well... I was thinking about how to say it all properly. I mean, I can show her everything in person here in the palace. That's the easiest way to explain, right?"

"Oh, you do give me a headache with your rash, thoughtless actions."

"But I *did* give it some thought!"

"Yes, yes, of course you did. In any event—Lady Euphyllia? Do you understand how the princess can addle the senses? She's like a powerful drug."

"...Yes. I can't deny it."

So I was addictive, was I? Well, I wasn't about to deny that. After all, I realized that well enough myself, so I could understand Ilia's apprehensions.

"Lady Euphyllia. First and foremost, I can assure you that the princess's offer is in good faith. Her intentions may not be *purely* altruistic, but she is acting out of consideration for you."

"Yes, I realize that..."

"But that is beside the point. The question is whether you understand just how potent a drug she is."

"...What do you mean exactly?" Euphie frowned.

She didn't seem to fully comprehend what Ilia meant—yet her reaction served as proof that Ilia's fears had been well-founded.

"The princess's study of magicology and her inventions, too, are wonderful things. Even considering only her Thermal Pot here, I'm a sure a great many potential uses spring to mind, yes?"

"Yes, it does seem like a wonderful invention."

"Indeed. If it came into general use, it could greatly improve people's lives. But that's where the problem lies."

"...Hmm?" Euphie was lost now.

Well, Ilia did have a point there. As wonderful as my magical tools were in and of themselves, there was no denying how addictive they could be.

Watching Euphie's reaction, Ilia breathed a gentle sigh and closed her eyes. "Once you've used it, you'll never be able to forget that comfort. You won't be able to go back to how things were before. In other words, it's a one-way street."

"That's going a little too far, don't you think?" I protested.

"It's like asking if you can take fire back from a civilization after teaching them how to use it," Ilia responded, completely ignoring me.

Euphie fell deep into thought, cupping her chin in her hand. Finally, seemingly having made up her mind, she glanced back up. "...Ah, I see. Hence a 'one-way street.' Experiencing these tools is a kind of point of no return to life as you knew it before."

"Yes, precisely. Magical tools are *too* convenient. The world that the princess envisions is difficult for us to comprehend, and once you arrive there, it's even more difficult to leave. By that time, you'll know for yourself just how wonderful it is."

I could understand what Ilia was trying to say. My inventions, the products of my magicology research, were based on ideas and concepts that didn't exist in this world. But civilization had developed in a different way here due to the existence of that magic. It was also the reason the authority of the noble and royal houses would never decline.

But at the same time, the existence of magic meant that other technologies hadn't developed as far as in my past life. That was why my inventions attracted so much attention—and why many considered them heretical. Just as how they had insisted no one could use magic to fly.

There were things that were common sense in the context of this civilization. Here, the knowledge I possessed was alien. I brought concepts and ideas that no one here had ever before seen. That was why I had argued that my magicology had the potential to overshadow any negative rumors about Euphie's broken engagement.

"So I don't recommend going down this path lightly," Ilia concluded.

Meanwhile, Euphie still seemed unsure.

The mood was getting dark, so I clapped my hands together. "Well, we can think about all that later. You're tired, aren't you, Euphie? Let's get some rest!"

I rose to my feet and picked Euphie up once more.

My guest must have been deep in thought, as her reaction was delayed by a split second. She began to resist only after falling into my arms.

"L-Lady Anis! This again...?!"

"Good night, Ilia! See you tomorrow!"

"Yes, good night, Princess. You too, Lady Euphyllia."

I ran through the corridors of the detached palace while Euphie was still flailing indignantly in my arms.

At first anyway. Realizing that her efforts were futile, she soon fell quiet. I adjusted her position and flashed her a smile.

"Don't worry, really. I won't do anything."

"..."

"You really don't trust me, do you...?"

If I had asked Ilia, we probably could have had an extra room prepared right away. She was so frustratingly capable. But I didn't want to leave Euphie by herself right now. She had caught my interest.

While I was thinking, I arrived at my room. I set Euphie down and moved to open the door. My bedroom was luxurious, as to be expected for royalty, with a bed more than large enough for two people to sleep in comfortably.

The table was piled high with books and other papers, while a set of huge clothes-filled closets and miscellaneous magical tools like Thermal Pots stood out, too.

Those magical devices were all re-creations of everyday items I remembered from my past life. For example, there was one called a Hair Dryer. I usually let Ilia take care of maintaining my appearance, but when she wasn't available, I had to see to it myself.

Euphie was staring around at those magical tools, her curiosity piqued.

"Now, Euphie. Let's get changed! I'll help you get undressed!"

"No, uh, I can't let you do that, Lady Anis…!"

"Come on, it's fine."

I knew how difficult it was to take off a dress by yourself. That was why I didn't like wearing them myself, although a member of the royal family just had to grin and bear it sometimes.

On other occasions, I usually wore custom-made clothes that combined features from the uniforms of knights and maids. The end result was almost like the military uniforms I remembered from my past life.

Regardless, that was why I had to help Euphie get changed. She resisted at first but reluctantly let me get to work.

I had to take care so as not to wrinkle her dress. The fabric looked expensive and was wonderful to the touch, as befitting a member of the House of Magenta.

"Ah, here. This is one of my nightgowns, but you can use it. It might be a little small on you, though."

I was a little on the short side, and Euphie was slightly taller than I was. She had a breathtakingly beautiful figure, with modest breasts that were actually perfectly proportioned to her slender frame. Was she the personification of the golden ratio, perhaps?

As for me? Ilia often teased me for being so short. Not that I cared, though…

"All right. I'll get changed, too; why don't you get into bed?"

"…All right."

Now that she was dressed for sleep, Euphie made herself comfortable. Maybe she was tired of resisting my suggestions.

I quickly changed into a nightgown, too, a different color than the one I had lent Euphie, and turned off the lights.

The room was plunged into darkness all at once, and I poured some magical energy into a device I had installed near the bed. Shortly afterward, a faint light illuminated the room.

Once the light was working, I turned to Euphie, who was lying in bed and squinting at me warily.

Flashing her a smile, I crept under the covers and beckoned her over.

"Come on, make yourself at home, Euphie!"

"...Excuse me."

Euphie was lying down on the mattress at a distance. The dim light was enough to illuminate both of our faces.

I studied her features once again. Her face was truly beautiful, the kind I could never grow tired of. Only then did I notice that she seemed uncomfortable under my gaze.

"Sorry, sorry. Bet it's hard to sleep with me staring at you like that."

"...What...?"

"Hmm?"

"...What are...you?" Euphie asked in a small voice.

It was an abstract question, and I wasn't entirely sure how to answer. Her expression was tinged with anxiety and consternation.

I forced a smile. "I'm me. An eccentric princess and the kingdom's troublemaker. A crazy, outlandish, unsolvable mystery."

"...There is much I could say, but I shan't."

"Is it really that strange? I mean, I've been shamelessly kind to you, don't you think?"

Perhaps I had been on the mark there, as Euphie fell silent. Nonetheless, she didn't lower her gaze, as though she were trying to peer through me. I felt like letting out an instinctive chuckle.

"I guess there's a lot of reasons why I'm doing this. I like you as a person, but I'm also pretty shrewd. I could string together all sorts of explanations, but none of them seem important to me right now."

"...They don't?" Euphie whispered back uncertainly.

I nodded, before averting my gaze and staring at the ceiling.

"I think people are driven by emotion, mainly. We laugh, we get sad, we get angry. That's why I can't just leave you."

"...Why not?"

"Because you don't strike me as the kind of person who knows how to do any of those!" I declared, turning back to her.

I startled when I saw how shocked she was. Only then, seeing her reaction, could I bring myself to relax.

"I've been watching you from afar, more than you know."

"...You have?"

"Yes. You're always so perfect. Smiling like a role model to everyone—and completely expressionless when emotion isn't called for. You're the perfect young noblewoman! Maybe that's why...when I found you there...I couldn't just ignore what was going on..."

"...I'm confused. Do you mean when you crashed into the party venue?"

"I mean, you weren't picture-perfect then. Or now. You've been crying and getting angry. You may be able to suppress your emotions, but I'm sure it's difficult for you."

Euphie was perfect. As our next queen, as the daughter of a duke, she was flawless. Her refined mannerisms, her quality education, her abundant talent. She was, by every measure, everything she ought to be.

But what if that perfection was wounded? What if it lost its meaning? What would she think of herself, then? What would she have left? Her talent, her spirit, the depth of the effort that she poured into everything would still be there. But if she was to lose sight of the goal she had worked so hard to achieve, what would she do next?

"So what I'm saying is that you need to do your best to feel those emotions for yourself. Do what *you* want. Because when I see you, it looks to me like you aren't able to do that. So I couldn't just ignore you."

"...That's your reason?"

"There's more to it, sure. I acted partly on instinct, partly by design. But most of all, I wanted to help you work out what you really, *really* want. That's the most important reason."

I reached under the covers and touched Euphie's hand. She pulled back slightly at first but then relaxed.

And so I pulled her to me in a warm embrace, let her bury her face in my chest, and patted her on the back.

"You did your best. So now it's time to get some rest."

"…"

With her face pressed against me, I couldn't read her expression. But I did notice she was weakly holding on to my clothes.

She didn't try to push me away. I closed my eyes with my arms still around her.

The trembling in her body gradually faded, and she drifted off to sleep. Only when I was sure she was slumbering did I allow myself to doze off, too.

* * *

The day after Euphie arrived at the detached palace, I was preparing to visit Duke Magenta.

Euphie had returned home ahead of me. After all, she had to change her clothes and get ready to move in with me properly, so she had arranged to be picked up in the morning while there were still few people out and about.

"Your Highness, please pay attention to your attire. You wouldn't want to offend the duke."

"Yes, yes. I know."

Ilia gave me a deep bow, then led me to my closet. I could only give an exaggerated sigh as she advised me on formal dress.

"I've been entrusted with Duke Magenta's beloved daughter, and there's the whole issue with Allie, too, so I'm willing to at least *try* to play along with expectations."

"Ah…! I can hardly believe that our wild, uncontrollable Princess Anisphia is being so docile for once…! I could die tomorrow fulfilled…!" Ilia exclaimed like an actress in an opera.

"You are so melodramatic."

With that, she quickly returned to her usual stoic, expressionless demeanor. "That being said, perhaps you should take a bath first?"

What was with those dramatic shifts in personality...?

"We'll choose a dress for you after you've bathed, and see to your makeup, too. Ah, and then—"

"You do come alive whenever you get to dress me up, don't you, Ilia?"

To be clear, *I* wasn't a fan of all this fancy dress. I only ever put myself through this when there was a social gathering that simply couldn't be avoided. Maybe I hated the extravagant clothing because of the association with those formal events?

Ilia nodded across at me, her expression still unreadable. "Let's use some flowers. People adore flowers. You used to, too."

"...Yes, yes, I know. Let's just get this over with."

I didn't have enough energy to argue with her, so I nodded back with a forced smile. And before I knew it, I was transformed into the image of a lovable young lady.

I would have resisted in the past, but now I knew there was no point, so I let Ilia do what she had to.

When I glanced at myself in the mirror, my face was so heavily painted that I hardly even recognized myself. Ilia's enthusiasm was incredible, truly—similar, perhaps, to my passion for magic. Looking at it that way, I found I could endure the hardship of having to make myself look pretty.

All of a sudden, I laid eyes on Ilia in the mirror. She might have been approaching her thirties, but her skin still had a youthful luster. She didn't seem at all old. In fact, she had hardly changed from my earliest memories of her.

On the contrary, her beauty seemed to have become only more refined with time. She was both a blessing to the eyes and one of those rare individuals I could easily get along with. I was truly fortunate to have her as my personal maid.

"You're beautiful, Ilia," I said.

"You tease. It's only because you gave me an invention to maintain my looks."

"I mean it. I've thought so since I was a child. That's why I worked so hard to create it."

"Ah, that brings back memories. I remember when you started bolting through the castle one day all of a sudden."

"Oh… Do you mean when you caught me and held me from behind?"

"Yes. That's when it all started. You started building your magical devices after that and managed to injure yourself more times than I can count. You would come back covered in cuts and bruises." Ilia's voice was fond as she tied my hair back.

She was referring to my past blunders—shared memories between the two of us.

At the time, I had just rediscovered my memories of my past life, and I had been so excited to know that the power of magic really did exist in this world. But then, of course, I had to face the fact that I couldn't use that magic myself. And then I had set about building my magical devices. Ilia had always been there for me. What would have become of me without her? I couldn't help but wonder. I quickly realized, however, that I was dwelling on those thoughts perhaps too much and pouted my lips.

"It's true that there were many failures, but there can be no success without making mistakes."

"In that case, my failure was that I didn't leave you." In the mirror, Ilia's mouth was unusually relaxed, almost a smile.

My eyes opened wide. It was a rare sight, this maid showing any sign of emotion.

"…And what kind of success did that bring you, Ilia?"

"This moment now."

I was so embarrassed that I had to murmur, "…You're exaggerating again."

That wasn't something to say so proudly. Nonetheless, Ilia began to giggle, even letting out a laugh.

I puffed my cheeks in frustration. "You have strange tastes, Ilia."

"Are you one to speak?" she asked, her smile widening.

She had been with me for more than a decade, but her appearance hadn't changed at all from how I remembered it. Even after all these years, she was still the same Ilia. I couldn't exactly say it aloud, but I was grateful to have her with me.

I thought of her like an elder sister, though she would likely be overwhelmed if I told her that.

Of course, she wasn't really my sister. Maybe more of a partner or a friend?

While I was musing about our relationship, Ilia had stopped tying my hair and begun to curl it around her finger playfully. She would often play with my unruly hair like this.

"...What is it?"

"Oh, I just thought how nice it is to be here. So marriage isn't the only path to happiness that a woman can choose."

"Ah... Right, about that..." I was at a temporary loss for words.

Ilia continued to stoke my head, letting my hair fall from her fingers. "Don't fret. My family name carries little weight, and I was also a pawn in a political marriage. It's no exaggeration to say that I am now, in a sense, married to you, Your Highness. Thanks to you, I have a good life," she said proudly, as though fully satisfied.

I, on the other hand, found my expression turning sour as I recalled her family.

Ilia was the daughter of a viscount. Her parents were particularly power hungry and had sought a marriage for her that could increase their social standing. Sending her to work as an attendant at the royal palace had been part of those plans.

No doubt they had hoped she might catch the eye of an heir to a house of means—if possible, an influential member of the nobility.

And those shallow intentions had led her here. That was when I first met her. Her parents had been frustrated that she had yet to find a partner, so when I heard they were trying to force her into an unwanted engagement, I went to great lengths to keep her with me.

And so, after many twists and turns, we arrived at where we were now. I had taken advantage of the situation to involve her in my magicology research, though I couldn't say whether that had been for the best.

At first, Ilia's family had welcomed my offer to take her into my employ. But after I relinquished my claim to the throne, they withdrew their good graces. I wasn't particularly fond of them, so as far as I was concerned, that wasn't a great loss.

Looking back on it all made me feel rather awkward. Ilia said she didn't mind, as she had always had a somewhat frigid relationship with her family. That was why she had stopped using her family name. She said she had practically been disowned, so I tried my best not to bring up the subject.

To me, she was simply Ilia. It didn't matter who her family was. I brought her here because I liked her for who she was. If that brought her happiness, all the better.

"Life is going to get even more exciting, Ilia. You'll stay with me, won't you?"

"As you wish, Your Highness. Although I won't hesitate to throttle you if need be."

I broke into laughter at her response. She was the reason I was here today. I couldn't thank her enough.

"Heh-heh, a perfect princess disguise... Thank you, Ilia!"

"What are you saying? You *are* a princess," she said, making a joke to hide her embarrassment.

We engaged in some more light conversation as I completed my preparations, before boarding a carriage to take us to Duke Magenta's residence in true princess style. Ilia sat across from me as my escort. It was difficult to relax; I missed my usual knight-inspired clothes.

The dukes of the House of Magenta belonged to an ancient lineage. They had a long history of a direct relationship to the royal family, although diluted by the ages. The dukes of Magenta were among the most venerated members of the nobility and had served the kings of Palettia as loyal vassals for generations. I had heard that Duke Grantz was a childhood friend of my father's, and the two had spent much time together during their youth.

Through this connection, I had even gone to play at the Magenta estate several times as a child. This had all been before Allie and I had become estranged.

Ever since our social positions had become more firmly established, we had grown somewhat distant from the Magentas. To be honest, I was a little reluctant to return there. I might have been dressed like royalty, but I wanted to tear all the finery off of me. Yet that wasn't an option where we were headed.

I steeled my nerves, trying to convince myself that this was my first official visit. That was when the gates to the Magenta estate came into view.

"Here we go, Ilia."

"Indeed, Your Highness."

As I stepped down from the carriage with Ilia attending to me, a line of maids led by an old butler bowed their heads in unison, each with perfect elegance and refinement.

"Welcome, Princess Anisphia."

"Thank you. I'm impressed. The Magentas are certainly worthy of their reputation."

"Your presence is a great honor, Your Highness. The duke is waiting for you inside. This way, please."

I was visiting as a princess today, so I reminded myself to behave appropriately. I could already feel my smile freezing somewhat, but as my visit was partly supposed to serve as an apology from the royal family, I would have to put up with it. I was a princess today—a princess.

With the greetings out of the way, the butler led me into the duke's mansion. As we passed through door after door, I was taken by the building's grandeur. It was certainly worthy of a family with such a long and distinguished history.

We were led into a drawing room, where we found Euphie, Duke Grantz, and a peaceful-looking woman waiting for us. The woman was Duchess Nerschell Magenta, the wife of Duke Grantz and Euphie's mother. Her silver-colored hair was done up in a large bun—undone, it would probably spill all the way down her back.

Duchess Nerschell exuded the sort of beauty that comes with age. Her eyes were pale green, reflecting a strong core. The strength of her gaze was one of her most renowned characteristics.

Euphie took after her father, yet I had to recognize that she had the inner strength of both parents. Incidentally, Euphie was supposed to have a younger brother. Did he resemble his mother, perhaps?

It had been a long time since I had last seen Duchess Nerschell, so I found myself staring at her. At that moment, our eyes met. I would have to greet her so as not to be rude.

"Good morning, Miss Euphyllia, Duke Grantz. It's been a long time, Duchess Nerschell. It's a great pleasure to see you again," I said with a bow.

"Not at all," Duke Grantz said, stepping forward to welcome me in turn. "It's an honor to have you visit us, Princess Anisphia."

I glanced up, shaking my head. "I'm the one asking for Miss Euphyllia to join me. If anything, I should be offering my thanks. Above all, I want to apologize for my brother. This is an official apology on behalf of the royal family, but on a personal level, I also want to express my own regrets." I bowed my head again to give my condolences.

"Please raise your head, Princess Anisphia," the duke said.

"You were looking out for our dear Euphie," the duchess added. "After all you've done for her, we couldn't possibly expect you to apologize."

I looked up and sat down as they ushered me to a seat. Ilia stood behind me, while the duke, the duchess, and their daughter sat immediately across.

"I haven't seen you in so long, Duchess Nerschell. I'm glad to see you're doing well."

"Yes, the same goes for you, too, Princess Anisphia. How long has it been since you last visited us?" The duchess covered her mouth with her hand, letting out a cheerful chuckle.

Her eyes were so compassionate that I found myself swaying restlessly. I was too used to people being cruel and hard-hearted, not this level of kindness.

"I remember coming here as a child... But I had to maintain a certain distance after Miss Euphyllia's engagement to my brother was decided."

"Yes. I'd hoped it wasn't true, but it seems the arrangement with Prince Algard hasn't turned out. If anything, it would be more constructive to dismiss this outcome as inevitable now that everything has come to light." Duchess Nerschell was still wearing a smile, but I could feel the force of the pressure behind her words.

Duke Grantz's countenance was intimidating by its unreadability, but the duchess's smile was an aggressive one. Seeing these two, I could understand why some people said Miss Euphyllia was stern at times. It most certainly ran in her blood.

At that moment, my gaze met Duchess Nerschell's. She flashed me an amiable smile, but I felt a thrill of tension from it.

"My husband and Euphie have already told me about your proposal," the duchess said, as though to change the topic. "If that is what Euphie wants, I will be happy to let her join you."

I breathed a small sigh of relief and forced myself to sit up straight to clear my mind. This was going to be an important discussion, so I had to keep it together.

"I'm honored to hear that you've agreed to it. As a member of the royal family who knows what it's like to lose the respect of those around her, I would like to help redeem Miss Euphyllia's honor after this unfortunate event. I will assume full responsibility for your daughter and take good care of her. This I swear on the name of the royal house," I declared, staring straight at the three Magentas.

At this, Euphie seemed to have a strange cast to her eyes, while Duchess Nerschell's shoulders were trembling unusually.

Duke Grantz, likewise aware of their reactions, shrugged. "You're acting rather proper today, Princess Anisphia. I almost found myself laughing there when you swore that oath on the name of your family."

"D-Duke Grantz?!"

It had seemed totally out of character to me as well, but did he have to say that aloud?! I was trying my best here to act like a proper princess! Even Ilia let out a sigh behind my back!

No, I wasn't doing anything wrong. Huh? Out of the ordinary? Well, maybe for me, I was...

"Ugh, Duke Grantz... I'm trying to treat the situation with the dignity it deserves!"

"Do forgive us. I never dreamed to see you conduct yourself so respectably," the duke responded with another shrug and a faint grin.

Something about his reply struck me as vaguely mischievous. Ugh, to think that the duke would tease me so...

"Your sincerity is clear. Please take good care of Euphie for us."

"Yes! I'll love her dearly!" I answered with a cheerful smile, bowing my head once more.

Yes! If Euphie decided to join me, I would be able to push on with my research! Hee-hee-hee!

After all, I needed the cooperation of a capable magic user to make my inventions. I might have possessed such magic myself, but I was incapable of properly using it. That had been a major impediment thus far, hence why I had set about creating my magical devices. And now Euphie, a prodigious talent, would become my research assistant! The future of my work was bright!

I had let my excitement carry me away a little when I suddenly remembered. What would Euphie do about her studies at the Aristocratic Academy? After all that commotion the other day, I doubted she could just go back.

"By the way, Duke Grantz... How will Euphie be treated from now on? Such as at the Aristocratic Academy...?"

"We've yet to discuss how to deal with all this or her future position for that matter... But I think it is best for her not to return for the time being."

"Right. I thought so, too."

"I will have to discuss the details with His Majesty, but I'll let you know once it's all decided."

"I'll be waiting. Please let me know if there's anything I can do to help."

"Very well... In that case, please be at ease, Princess Anisphia."

"...That's rather mean, Duke Grantz. I'm trying to help here, you know?"

He did seem to be trying to be considerate to me, but did he think me incapable of behaving myself like a modest princess? Well, maybe that *was* beyond me. But if he wanted me to take it easy, I most certainly would!

I adjusted my posture to get comfortable, when Euphie and Duchess Nerschell suddenly started giggling. Hmph! Everyone knew I was a no-good princess anyway!

"Thank you for looking after our Euphie, Princess Anisphia," Duchess Nerschell said.

"Of course! Actually, I'll be asking a lot from her, so thank *you*!"

"Oh dear. Well then, I had better help pack her things. Euphie? Let's go."

"Yes, Mother. Excuse me, Lady Anis."

Euphie and Duchess Nerschell curtsied before leaving the parlor to prepare for the move.

As I watched them go, Duke Grantz called out to me: "Thank you again, Princess Anisphia."

"There's no need for that, Duke Grantz. I'm grateful to have Euphie assisting me."

The duke wavered slightly at this response, although his gaze remained piercing, enough to send a chill down my spine. It was like he was trying to see deep inside me.

"...I didn't think you had a good impression of me," the duke said.

"Huh? Why wouldn't I?"

I tilted my head to one side at this unexpected declaration. Had he really thought that? But why?

Duke Grantz was, in a way, my father's right-hand man. He wielded a great deal of political power, but more importantly, he was my father's friend, his confidant, and an important ally. I had no reason to think negatively of him. I tilted my head to the other side in bewilderment.

At that moment, the duke burst into laughter. All I could do was stare back at him wide-eyed.

"You haven't changed at all, Princess Anisphia."

"Oh...? Is that so?"

"Indeed. Since you announced you had no intention of marrying, you've been meeting nothing but success in your accomplishments. His Majesty hasn't known what to do with you for a long time now. I've seen that firsthand." The duke's voice was filled with nostalgia as he lay bare emotions that he normally kept hidden.

I, on the other hand, was simply confused. Why would he reveal this side of himself to me of all people, instead of his own daughter?

"Are you certain *you* didn't have such a great impression of *me*?"

"Ah. I wonder," Duke Grantz demurred with a bold grin.

In the end, I had no idea what he was thinking. I frowned back at him, not fully satisfied by his response.

"You're fine as you are, Princess Anisphia. Please take good care of Euphie."

"Ah..."

No, I wasn't at all satisfied, but at least he didn't seem to think too poorly of me now. I decided not to press any further.

"In that case, I'll leave you to it. Please excuse me. I have some business I must attend to."

"Oh, of course. Thank you for taking the time to see me."

Right. The duke was a busy man and didn't have a lot of free time. He was probably needed elsewhere, especially given the situation with Allie. The duke gave me a formal bow, leaving me alone with Ilia.

I relaxed my shoulders and let out a sigh, when Ilia turned her attention to me.

"You're making too many mistakes, Your Highness. You should at least wait until we've returned to the palace before you let down your guard."

"Right, right. You're always finding fault, Ilia."

"I'm honored you think so."

I hadn't meant that as a compliment... But I did feel a little more comfortable after this exchange. A butler in the employ of the House of Magenta brought us a pot of tea as we waited.

Ilia busied herself asking the butler about tea, then about Euphie. Given that she was the only attendant at my palace, she would be responsible for taking care of Euphie, so she no doubt had many things she wanted to confirm. I could look after myself, but Euphie might require more attention.

I had nothing to do, so I simply listened into the pair's conversation as I waited.

"Thank you for your patience, Lady Anis," Euphie called out when she returned.

"Are you ready?"

"Yes. I don't have many belongings to begin with...," she said with a soft smile, though her brow was furrowed in a frown.

Was something bothering her, perhaps?

I found myself turning toward Duchess Nerschell, who let out a troubled chuckle.

Huh? What was going on?

"Did something happen?"

"...I had a small quarrel with my little brother."

"Oh? About what?"

Euphie's brother hadn't joined us, so I had no idea why the two of them might be arguing.

Euphie, seeing that I didn't understand, flashed me a forced smile. "I'm sorry, Lady Anis. It's a family matter..."

She often seemed to be wearing this expression lately, as though she was having difficulty knowing what to do with her face. What had happened while she was packing? I glanced toward Duchess Nerschell, but she merely cleared her throat and returned my gaze.

"My son doesn't like being apart from his elder sister. He wasn't very happy about her going to join you at the palace, so he put up a bit of a fight..."

"Ah... I see..."

I was in a completely different position from Allie, but it made sense that Euphie's brother would be worried about her safety there.

But she would be much safer with me than she would be staying here, from what I could see. She wouldn't be staying at the royal palace, either, but rather at my villa. She would have little cause to come into contact with strangers.

That was no doubt why Duke Grantz had given his approval. But maybe it was a little much to ask Euphie's younger brother to understand. Yes, it was a difficult situation...

"He's still rather immature, which is why I didn't ask him to join us. I'm sorry to worry you, Princess Anisphia."

"Not at all. This is the royal family's responsibility, too. We caused this problem in the first place."

I couldn't say I didn't understand how Euphie's brother must have felt. My family was the underlying cause of this mess, after all.

Perhaps having read my thoughts, Duchess Nerschell shook her head. Her expression tightened as she addressed me in a slightly aggrieved voice. "This is a good opportunity for my son, too, so he can learn to spend time apart from his sister. I'm sorry if this seems somewhat feckless, but I'm truly grateful to you for taking her in."

"It's fine! Please raise your head, Duchess Nerschell! Don't worry, please! This benefits me, too, really!"

The duchess was bowing so deeply that I nearly panicked. I was just acting according to my own whims, so all this pomp wasn't necessary.

"Don't worry. Euphie and I will achieve great things, and she'll be able to reenter high society again before you know it! That way, we'll be able to restore her honor. I'm sure her brother will appreciate that, too."

"Oh, my daughter is truly fortunate to have you, Princess Anisphia…"

"Mother…," Euphie murmured, softening.

With that, the atmosphere in the room relaxed. Duchess Nerschell flashed her daughter a smile before grasping her hands in her own.

"Euphie. No matter how far away you are, I wish you happiness. Your father and I share responsibility for this state of affairs, as we raised you thinking only to prepare you to be our future queen. Please don't worry about us. Just look after yourself." Her gentle voice was filled with strong affection.

Ilia and I watched on as Euphie gave her mother a short nod.

And so we set off in our carriage back to the detached palace, Euphyllia staring outside the window until her family home disappeared out of sight.

CHAPTER 3

The Reincarnated Princess's Magicology Lesson

"Hmm, now that that's over, it's time for a break!"

A few days after Euphie officially moved into the detached palace with me, things had finally settled down. Meanwhile, everyone over at the royal palace seemed to be in a state of panic because of the broken engagement— at least according to Ilia, when I asked her about the situation.

The instigators of the whole incident, Allie and the sons of the other nobles, had been suspended from school and brought in for questioning, and that had resulted in a great commotion.

I couldn't help but wonder what would happen to them, but we here at the villa would be unaffected. While all that was going on, I had decided to busy myself in my workshop to take a breather.

My workshop was filled with blueprints and prototypes of new magical tools. I didn't even let Ilia in here without my permission, so the room often got rather messy.

I wasn't intentionally trying to clutter it; I would hardly even notice the mess building until Ilia started expressing her disapproval. I knew she didn't mean anything by it, though—she was simply more tidy than I was.

"Now that Euphie's here, why don't we try a new experiment? What should we make...?"

Hmm... I pulled out the notebook I used for jotting down ideas and diagrams of things I remembered from my past life.

I was a foreigner in this world. Ever since I had regained memories of my past life, I had felt my thoughts and values shifting closer to what they used to be.

But while I might suddenly remember things from my past life, those memories could drift away just as easily. That was why I had my notebook—to make as detailed a record as possible while I still could.

I wanted to leave as huge a mark on this world as I could during my time here. Fortunately, I doubted I would be departing anytime soon.

"Hmm... We should at least refrain from any experiments that would draw too much attention, given the circumstances. So we'll have to hold off on anything that requires a lot of materials... Maybe I should ask Euphie, make sure we're on the same page and all...?"

Alone with my thoughts, my brain was turning in circles, when there came a knock at the door.

"May I come in, Your Highness?" Ilia called suddenly.

I was startled out of my sea of thoughts and called back to her, "Yes?"

"Excuse me." With my permission, Ilia stepped foot into my workshop.

Euphie entered a second later, her eyes opening wide as she took in her surroundings.

"Welcome, Euphie. This is my workshop."

"Pardon me... So this is where you work, Lady Anis?"

"Yes. There are quite a few prototypes lying around, so make sure you don't accidentally touch anything, all right?"

After my warning, Euphie tiptoed into the room with trepidation.

I doubted we would have any problems, as I kept all the really dangerous items in a safe place. It was just that sometimes, when I pulled an all-nighter, I let myself get carried away and ended up producing some rather inelegant items.

I had placed an extra seat on the other side of my desk. Euphie sat down there while Ilia began to prepare some tea. It was practically business as usual for this workshop, except for Euphie's presence.

"Everything all right?"

"I just thought, seeing as I'm your assistant, maybe I could help with something..."

"Ah, so you're feeling better now? Have you settled in? It must be hard getting used to a new environment."

"I'm fine, really. I'd rather be doing something than sitting around idly."

I'd been seeing Euphie's troubled expression a lot lately. But I suppose it was true that not having anything to do might be unsettling. If she said she was ready, then it was probably time to involve her!

"All right, then. First of all, I'd like to make sure we're on the same page."

"The same page...?"

"Yes. You know I can't use magic, right?"

Euphie seemed unsure how to respond at first, but she slowly nodded.

Most nobles in the Kingdom of Palettia were capable of using magic. Essentially, it was one's magical aptitude, rather than talent or skill, that tended to determine one's social status.

I was completely useless in that respect. I *did* possess magic, but I was incapable of wielding it. According to my research, that was an inborn trait of mine, not something I could change with hard work.

"Well, I have a working hypothesis as to the underlying cause, but still..."

"...Huh? H-hold on, Lady Anis."

"Hmm? Yes?"

"A working hypothesis for why you can't use magic? I've never heard that before..."

"Of course not. I haven't had a chance to present it yet."

Euphie was staring across at me in suspicion. I had no intention of actually publicizing my theory. It would probably only cause yet another uproar.

That was why only a few people, my father being one of them, knew about the results of my research. I had also discussed them, to some extent, with the directors of a few institutions that studied spirits and magic.

"In other words, what seems like common sense to one of us might be totally foreign to the other. You see? That's why we need to share our ideas, to make sure we understand each other. We won't be able to proceed otherwise."

"...I see. I understand." Euphie nodded, her expression difficult to read.

I was so pleased to have an attentive listener that I leaped to my feet, brimming with energy. I quickly pulled up a movable blackboard.

I was so excited that I felt like a cram school teacher. As I prepared to dive into my explanations, Ilia started pouring out some cups of tea. *Well done, Ilia!*

"Now, then. Let's start with the basic premises behind magic. Magic is performed with the help of spirits. Isn't that right, my clever young Euphie?"

"Clever— What?"

"Just play along!"

"Er...?" At first, Euphie seemed puzzled by the ease with which I had adopted the mannerisms of a professor, but she soon regained her composure. "Um... Magic works through intermediary spirits that exist all throughout the world. It's essentially a trade—you give your magical energy, and they produce a magical effect. I was taught that everyone has different levels of affinity with different spirits, and that determines one's overall aptitude for using magic."

"Indeed. That part is common knowledge."

An exemplary response—as expected of a renowned genius. She must have been an enthusiastic student at the academy, I thought with a pang of sadness. She was such a good person at heart.

Right, back to the matter at hand. Euphie was correct in her explanation of how magic functioned. In this world, magic was conducted through spirits, and there was a rich diversity of different spirits.

First, there were the primordial spirits, the spirits of light and darkness that were said to have been in existence since the creation of the world. Next came the four great spirits of fire, water, earth, and wind, which were said to have been born when the creator gods forged the world. After that came various other types of spirits that were generally described as subtypes of the aforementioned four. These innumerable spirits were what gave the nobles of the Kingdom of Palettia their status and power.

"By magical aptitude," I said, "you mean one's compatibility with those spirits, yes? In other words, that's the criterion that decides one's skill at wielding magic?"

"Yes. That's what we learned at the academy."

"Excellent! But here's the thing. I've delved into the topic a step further!"

"What do you mean?" Euphie asked, tilting her head to one side.

Her understanding of magic was essentially the commonsense one. But I was a more unconventional scholar when it came to magicology.

With a nod, I raised a finger into the air for emphasis. "Let's get to the heart of the problem, Euphie. Do you know what precisely determines one's affinities with spirits?"

"...That's... I don't know. Wouldn't that be one's physical and mental constitution? Or their bloodline?"

"Hee-hee-hee. Sorry, sorry. That was a mean question."

She was right; one's overall affinity was unique to them. In some cases, people did inherit their abilities from their parents, but that wasn't guaranteed. As such, no one had a clear answer when it came to explaining precisely what determined one's spiritual affinities.

"But why can't *I* use magic? I had to investigate and find the underlying reason. So I began my research trying to get to the heart of magical affinities."

"...Forgive me for asking this, but is it really true that you can't...?" Euphie asked awkwardly, having worked up her resolve.

That topic risked derailing the conversation, but I couldn't afford to not answer. It looked like she hadn't wanted to broach the question, probably trying to be sensitive.

"I can't. Not one iota. I can't sense any indication of spirits at all."

"...I see."

"I know other people can sense the presence and existence of spirits, and that's what we mean by *affinity*, but I have no idea what it feels like. I've been this way since I was born, so there's nothing I can do about it."

I couldn't know for certain, but it seemed that the magically able could sense the presence of spirits nearby. And if you could sense them, you could channel them to use magic, for good or ill.

All that was to say that seeing as I couldn't sense spirits, I couldn't use magic. I remembered being told that the true cause for all this was that

I hadn't offered sufficient prayer to them, so they were refusing to lend me their power, or something like that. That was also how people here understood it. The element of prayer was especially significant when it came to using magic.

"To use magic, it is important to pray to spirits. You need to convey to them a clear image of what kind of magic you want to use. Isn't that right?"

"Yes. It's recommended to try chanting at first, to deepen your awareness of their power. Experts can often skip that step, but you do regularly see chanting in large rituals."

I nodded with satisfaction at this response. To activate magic, the first step was to sense the presence of spirits. Next, the magic user had to convey an image of how they intended to use the spell. Finally, they had to direct sufficient magical energy to activate the technique. That was the entire process in a nutshell.

And since I had stumbled at the very first step, I couldn't cast anything. In other words, the problem was that I couldn't sense spirits.

"So *why* can't I sense the presence of spirits? If we want to find the answer, we have to ask ourselves, what *are* spirits?"

"…They simply are, no?" Euphie asked with a frown.

Technically correct, but that wasn't what I meant. I smiled weakly.

"People say they've been around since the beginning of time, but are they living creatures? Or are they embodiments of natural phenomena? What do you think, Euphie? Can you explain the logic and reasoning behind the existence of spirits?"

"That's…"

"Spirits have existed for so long that people take them for granted. No one questions them. But for me, spirits are a mystery. That's why I set about studying them."

My research had uncovered that while different spirits had different attributes, spirits were commonly found floating in the air. As far as could be measured, they had no physical substance. In other words, they were born from nature itself. They had no will of their own—at best, they reacted instinctively, as certain other organisms did. But it was safe to say they didn't act consciously.

"The important thing to remember is that spirits feed on magical energy."

"You mean they can't live without it?"

"Exactly. That's what's interesting about them. They operate on instinct. They don't have a sense of will, as we do. Just as we require air and food to live, they rely on magical power."

Euphie's jaw was dropping as she listened to my explanation. I chuckled; it was really quite funny.

So why did spirits require magical power? Why did magical techniques activate when they were fed? With that question in mind, I began to investigate the activation itself.

"So we've established that spirits feed on magical energy. In that case, what *is* magical energy? Euphie, any ideas?"

"…Magical energy is magical energy… I assume that's wrong, isn't it?"

"Indeed."

"Can I ask something? What do *you* think magical energy is, Lady Anis?"

"An excellent question. I like your enthusiasm. So what *is* magical power? To use a metaphor, I would say that it's like…intangible blood spilling out from the soul."

"…Intangible…blood?"

"It's just an analogy, but it should make it easier to visualize."

Why did spirits require magical power? The conclusion I had reached was that it was their source of sustenance.

The next question to come to mind pertained to the nature of magical energy. I regarded it as an intangible blood of sorts.

"How did you come up with *that* idea…?" Euphie asked with wonder.

Yes, well. I'd had a hint. Or rather, it was precisely because of who I was that I had come to this conclusion.

I mean, I had been reincarnated. This body of mine was a product of this world, but its contents weren't. That was the secret behind my research here.

Perhaps it was precisely *because* I had been reincarnated that I couldn't use magic?

That had been my initial working hypothesis. I felt a little nostalgic thinking back to it all.

"Each person has different affinities. Sometimes they are inherited, sometimes they aren't. So if each person has an individual form of magical power, where does it come from?"

There were no rules when it came to one's affinity with spirits. Yes, blood played a role, but that wasn't the whole story. In that case, there had to be a more fundamental reason. If the reason was that I was effectively alien to this world, that led to only one answer.

"We can say, then, that the deciding factor for spiritual affinity lies in the soul."

Euphie listened to my theory, her expression serious. I drew a simple diagram on the blackboard to explain. This was turning more and more into a lecture, and I was perhaps letting myself get carried away by the moment.

"Magical energy is an invisible spiritual force emanating from the soul. And spirits are incorporeal beings that exist out in the world. If we assume that spirits feed on magical energy, we can hypothesize that mental images and prayer are important to invoke magic."

"Is this your theory of exercising magic?"

"It is. Why does magic work as magic? Perhaps spirits are *converted* by magical energy? Or so I started wondering."

"Converted into techniques, you mean?"

"Yes. In other words, we can define magic as giving shape to an incorporeal spirit."

I wrote this down as a heading on the blackboard, then turned back to Euphie with a grin.

For her part, Euphie was astonished, as though she had just had a firsthand encounter with something she'd never seen before in her life.

In fact, this probably *was* all completely new to her. I had only been able to explain this theory to a very select number of individuals, and they had received it all with equal wonder.

"So spirits are *converted* into magic...? You're saying that magic isn't the result of spirits manifesting our prayers...?"

"That's the general belief. But I think my theory is more likely. Spirits don't have free will, they simply float through the world. Feeding them energy makes them transform, and that's what we call magic."

"But then, what happens to the spirits after they become magic?"

"They turn back to normal, I guess? Spirits are supposed to disappear after you cast anyway, right?"

Spirits had incorporeal bodies, so even once they lost the magical form given to them, there would be no problem. They never had any real physical substance to begin with.

"That makes sense, but still...," Euphie murmured, sinking deep into her own thoughts.

Well, it was about time we took a break. I needed a drink, and the tea Ilia had brewed would be getting cold.

Incidentally, I had already made a hypothesis about how much magical energy was required to produce an effect. Magical energy was like the blood of the soul and was necessarily modeled after the soul.

By my definition, magical energy was a form of power that spilled out from a vessel that we called the soul. There had to be a source of that power inside the soul. And if we thought of the soul as a vessel, then the purpose of magical power had to be to ensure that the soul didn't become depleted.

The soul never emitted more energy than it required, but any excess power could be expelled from the body. This surplus was what people recognized as magical energy. One's aptitudes and affinities were determined by the kinds of spirits that preferred that type of magical power, and that in turn determined how much energy was required to produce the desired effect.

"This is still just a hypothesis, but since spirits lack consciousness, they're instinctively drawn to magical energy. That's also why they submit to the will of the entity providing them with that power. So basically, according to my theory, spirits don't consciously respond to one's will or anything like that."

Euphie was more subdued now. But I had expected this kind of reaction and smiled.

The Kingdom of Palettia had a long history of belief in our friendship with spirits. That was where the people's belief system had been born—their faith that spirits were our neighbors and that we owed them our reverence.

My ideas were heretical to such believers, so I seldom shared them with others. Because there were a great many people who believed, at one level or another, in the basic principles of spiritualism in this country. And yet if Euphie was going to help collaborate on my research, this was something she needed to know.

"...I always considered magical energy and spirits to be facts of nature... I've never really given them much thought before."

"I only kept investigating out of necessity, but that's how I came up with this theory. If I could figure out how magic works, I could try to come up with a hypothesis as to why I can't use it."

To put it simply, my conclusion was that spirits didn't like my specific type of magical energy.

There was no doubt that I did possess magical energy, but I couldn't use it. Which brought me to my hypothesis: Spirits require magical energy as a form of sustenance.

They unconsciously seek out energy compatible with their own constitutions. This was what people understood as aptitude. For instance, an individual whose energy was favored by water spirits would have an aptitude for water magic. Essentially, one's aptitude was determined by the preferences of the various spirits.

"I should add in passing that I think the rise of the nobility and the royal family all began with contracts with spirits."

"Spirit covenants, you mean?"

That term carried some weight here in the Kingdom of Palettia.

According to my hypothesis, spirits didn't have their own free will. That said, there *were* exceptions to that rule: Elementals, great spirits that were born from accumulations of countless smaller ones. There were those who called such existences gods.

There were many stories of those who had entered into such pacts with great spirits and had been granted tremendous power in return. The noble and royal families who had founded the Kingdom of Palettia were said to have done precisely that, as was the first great king.

Lore and legends from various regions seemed to contain similar descriptions of Elementals conversing with people and acting according to their own free will. This, naturally, was inconsistent with the results of my research into the nature of spirits.

That was why I came up with this additional hypothesis. Elementals weren't simply a higher level of spirit; their existence had become so definite that they had developed their own will.

Of course, I would have liked to confirm all this with solid evidence, but those who entered into spirit covenants generally had extremely unusual values and a tendency to seclude themselves in remote parts of the world. I once asked my father to introduce me to one, but he turned me down. They received the protection of the state, but they wanted to be left alone except in emergencies.

"Those who enter into spirit covenants with Elementals supposedly possess powers beyond those of ordinary magic. That's why all countries have taken in such individuals."

"It is said that the Kingdom of Palettia was founded by nobles with such connections, too. The fact that our nobles can use magic is a remnant of the spirit covenants their ancestors entered into."

But that had all happened a long time ago, so there was no way to uncover the truth for certain, short of digging up some ancient records. Uncovering long-forgotten history was the dream of some, but my dreams lay elsewhere.

Given the kingdom's origins, the ability to use magic was incredibly highly valued—which was stifling to someone like me, who couldn't.

"I'm not sure if it's the bloodline of the ancients who entered into those covenants or the affinities of their magical energy that they're attuned to, though. But maybe we'll leave it at that for now. Shall we get back to the topic at hand?"

"We did get sidetracked, didn't we? Yes, please continue."

"I'm the one who went off topic. Well, spirits don't like my magical energy, and because of that, I can't call on them."

"Is that why you developed your magical tools?" Now that we had returned to the main topic, Euphie's expression reverted to its prior tense state.

I took another sip of the tea before continuing, "I *do* have magical energy, so I have to find a way to make effective use of it. And I've always wanted to use magic. I don't mind if that means doing it in a nontraditional way."

As an aside, the reason commoners couldn't use magic was that they possessed no vestiges of ancient spirit covenants. In the rare event that a commoner was born with the ability, the most likely explanation was simply that they were the illegitimate child of a nobleman.

On top of that, the Kingdom of Palettia had a long history. There were accounts of aristocrats choosing to abandon their noble status—and of others who had eloped to live with commoners. Considering all that, some exceptions were bound to occur.

Those factors could pose a bit of a problem, but that was a matter for another time.

"I don't have much natural talent, so I had to work hard to discover everything I have and get to the point where I am now."

"And that's how you developed your magical tools?"

"Exactly. I started by looking for ways to use magic that didn't have to involve spirits."

Excess magical energy ultimately dissipated upon being released from the body. If it wasn't consumed by spirits, it was essentially wasted. So I decided to research whether I could put it to any other use.

"I started by focusing on spirit stones. Of course, you already know about them, right?"

"Yes. Spirit stones are crystals of concentrated spirit power, found in places with lots of spirits or granted by a great spirit."

"Right. So I decided to try to figure out what they *really* are."

"Huh? Are they not what they seem?"

"I mean, they aren't just regular old stones, right? You can't understand them without knowing how they were created or the basic principles behind them."

"...I see. You approach everything with an analytical attitude, don't you, Lady Anis?" Euphie nodded in admiration.

I didn't think I had done anything special, though... Well, back to the topic at hand.

Spirit stones were crystalline rocks filled with spirit power. With these, even commoners could call on the power of spirits, albeit to a limited degree for limited results.

For example, a fire stone could only be used as a substitute for a fireplace. Water stones could produce water, but that was it. Wind stones could create wind, but they weren't powerful enough to enable flight. Earth stones could enrich the land, but they couldn't trigger tremors or earthquakes. In other words, their magic was relatively degraded.

"So the question is—how do spirit stones come to be? To put it simply, I think they're like the corpses of spirits."

"...Huh?" Euphie was unable to reply again—this was happening a lot today.

I hadn't been trying to elicit a reaction—I simply thought that comparison would be the easiest analogy to understand.

"Spirit stones are the end result, when a spirit solidifies into a material form, becoming a shadow of its former self. So in biological terms, they're like corpses..."

"...That may be a great discovery, but if you put it like that, people won't take it well," Euphie said dubiously.

I couldn't say I didn't understand, but I just couldn't think of a better way of phrasing it. Even calling them *fossils* didn't exactly make sense, as spirits had no physical form to begin with. And calling them *clumps* of spirits wouldn't exactly help people to understand, either.

Did describing them that way really sound so terrible? I suppose the elite magic users at the Ministry of the Arcane had frowned when I had explained it to them—although a few of them did hear me out.

"When I tried to dig down into the core of my ideas, I found that reality could be quite unforgiving. Unlike living organisms, the concept of death doesn't really apply to spirits, and they don't bear any grudges or resentments. Although, that might not necessarily be the case for Elementals, which do seem to have more of a conscious will."

"I see…" Euphie looked rather uncomfortable.

Well, that was a fairly normal reaction for one from this country. The important thing to note was that spirit stones were masses of materialized, concentrated spirits.

It was easy to locate spirit stones in places rich in nature and abundant in life. The Kingdom of Palettia had just the right balance of nature and human settlement for spirit stones to be found. In essence, it was an environment ideal for spirits, rich with humans who could sustain them with magical energy.

There were high-purity, high-quality spirit stones to be found in abundance in the countryside, but even without going out that far, you could easily mine enough to improve people's daily lives just outside regular villages and towns. That was why they were indispensable for the Kingdom of Palettia, both as everyday tools and a primary export. People were immensely grateful to have them.

"Ah, how nostalgic. I remember when you used a huge pile of wind stones and crashed straight into the castle wall," Ilia murmured all of a sudden as she prepared a fresh pot of tea.

I frowned at this. *There was no need to say that, Ilia…! Now Euphie seems scandalized, too!*

"You *crashed* into it…?" she asked.

"I thought my whole body would fall apart," I replied.

"It makes for an amusing story now, but it really did cause quite a stir," Ilia added.

Yet that mistake had helped me learn once and for all that I had zero aptitude for magic, and it cleared up my doubts about spirit stones. So in the end, everything turned out fine. I had figured out how spirit stones worked, and I would need a great many to freely use the kind of magic I wanted.

"So that's where my quest of trial and error began. It took me nearly a decade, but I've finally reached the point where I am today."

"Is that why people started calling you *Princess Peculiar*...?"

"Indeed. I really wanted to use magic. Even now, I'm still not satisfied. I can use some of the energy being released by my body through my magical tools, but I still need to develop more of them."

"I see... So why did you want me to become your assistant?" Euphie tilted her head to one side quizzically.

You could probably say that Euphie and I were complete opposites. The spirits had turned their back on me, yet they adored her. She truly had a high level of aptitude for magic in every sense.

"To see various kinds of magic in use. Also, because you seem to have a knack for every kind of magic there is without any impediment to your physical abilities. It's an unfair advantage. It's like you've broken the rules. You're a mystery."

"Broken the rules...? A-am I that strange?"

"I mean, there's something really strange about the fact that you even exist."

In fact, my research results showed that possessing too much magical energy could cause all kinds of harm—like diseases that were unique to this world.

Those diseases were all related in one way or another to one's magical energy. For example, there were cases where the sufferer's body couldn't release excess power, which placed a tremendous strain on their mental and physical health.

Magical energy could affect the body or mind in a wide range of ways, such as abnormal transformations when the balance was broken. When I told this to Euphie, her face turned deathly pale. She had a ridiculous number of aptitudes and tremendous magical energy reserves, too.

Such maladies occurred because magical power emanated from the soul, so if the balance between body and soul became unstable, either or both could suffer considerable damage.

From what I could tell, there seemed to be some similarity to what had been called *mental illness* in my past life. In this world, humans were more prone to these difficulties, which I assumed was the result of coexisting with spirits.

That was why a great many nobles here seemed to suffer from mental illness or physical ailments—because they were unable to properly release the magical energy building up inside their bodies. And when such power wasn't able to escape, it could cause symptoms almost like root rot in plants. When that happened, the soul could no longer withstand being saturated in magical energy. And of course, when that warped the soul, it brought about mental instability, while also putting excessive strain on the body.

This was a monumental discovery. However, I had yet to widely publicize it, nor had it taken off on its own. I couldn't afford to take it for granted without further evidence, and I wasn't a doctor. I was afraid that if I tried to pull back the curtain too soon, the rumors might get out of hand. As such, this was one of those matters I had left in my father's hands.

In fact, I had heard that my father had ordered further research be carried out to confirm whether my hypothesis was correct, and I was being credited for the initiative.

"But aren't you worried, if spirits are drawn to my magical energy? Couldn't I pose a danger?"

"The opposite is true, too. Those spirits could end up consuming too much of your magical energy, depleting what you need to stay healthy. That could end up causing illness or disability. You must be adored by the gods, because you've achieved a miraculous balance, Euphie. You could be the kind of genius who appears only once in a hundred—no, in a thousand years!"

"...I'm more surprised to hear that magical energy can cause illness than to be called a genius...," Euphie murmured, her complexion pale as she hugged her trembling body.

I was truly grateful to Duke Grantz and Duchess Nerschell for bringing up such a healthy young lady.

"In summary, it's best to have a good balance when it comes to magical energy. I'm sure you've heard they've started to examine your magical energy levels during routine health checkups, to see how much you have and how skilled you are at using it."

"Ah, so *that's* why they introduced those measures in magic classes at the academy..."

It was possible to prevent certain outcomes even without revealing the intent behind those measures. A few years after I had devised this theory, I heard that the academy had begun to measure each student's total level of magical energy and their skill level, too, to collect data and start measuring any abnormalities.

Of course, magical energy wasn't the only thing that could break someone's mind. If you went around blaming magic for everyone's ills, you would only invite persecution from those who possessed magical abilities in abundance. As such, my father was proceeding with this matter using great delicacy, I had heard.

"There have been cases where even wild, out-of-control children have become calmer and more stable after learning magic and increasing their skill level. But that doesn't solve every problem, and they still tend to take out their anger on others when things don't go well. So magical energy is just one contributing factor there."

"But it must be a big step forward to discover the cause." Euphie nodded in admiration.

I was genuinely happy to see that reaction. I was really getting into this lecture, but Ilia's stern glance told me to keep myself in check.

"So is this magicology? Investigating things like that?"

"No. This is just a by-product. I'm not a specialist, either, so most of what I do is conjecture. We'll need an expert to confirm it. After all, I may *study* magic, but I'm not a magic user or a doctor."

Ultimately, magicology was a discipline I had created to try to find a way to use magic, seeing as I had no other way of doing it. I drew knowledge from my past life to try to reproduce that science through my magical tools. At least, that had been my original goal, but it had led to a lot of secondary outcomes.

"For me, magicology is just another way of thinking about the world."

There were other researchers of magic, but their approaches were more like theology or religion, quite different from my own. Still, the findings I had announced had been well received by practicing magic researchers. In fact, they had seemed rather impressed.

My theory about imbalances between the body and one's innate magical energy was an eye-opener for them. I had even received personal thanks for my positive influence on other studies and the education of future researchers.

Hah! Thanks, I guess? Was I supposed to feel grateful for the praise of regular magic users? All that time, they had treated me like a troublemaker, like an idiot! Just looking back on it made me so angry!

They had mocked my magical tools relentlessly before! It was infuriating! I was still mad about it, really. I would never forgive those fools at the Ministry of the Arcane! I knew that not everyone there was like that, but honestly, I just hated those highbrow elites. I didn't want to have anything to do with them.

"...Lady Anis?" Euphie called out, sounding worried and pulling me back from the pool of dark emotion.

Whoops, that was close. I had to maintain a sense of normalcy.

The Ministry of the Arcane was a major political faction in the kingdom and had a powerful voice. That said, I really didn't like them. They regarded magic as a privilege of the nobility and looked down on commoners and everyone else who couldn't use it.

I *really* hated the idea of a chosen few individuals possessing special powers. I understood that being able to use magic was a symbol of status, but there had to be more to life than that. That might sound strange coming from someone who had always adored magic and dedicated herself to making tools with it, but in the end, what I did was also partially a hobby.

"Um, did we get off topic again? What was I saying?" I asked.

"You were talking about reconciling our understanding of magicology," Euphie responded. "About how we need to start with a clear understanding of the subject."

"Right. Somewhere along the line, we started talking about spirits and magical energy rather than magicology as such. Well, it *is* all kind of intertwined, though."

"The outside world might have heard the word *magicology*, but they don't know anything about what it really involves, right? But I've heard that you often go out to construction sites? Sewers, roads, highways, and the like...?"

"Ah. Well, that's kind of my father's fault..."

I had revealed to my father my hazy knowledge of sewers, and he had carefully considered the notion. Before I knew it, he had assigned me to the role of adviser and assistant on-site supervisor, all because I had told him that if we had underground sewers, we would be able to improve sanitation and the quality of the cityscape.

Also, I had argued that wastewater was a major cause of illness and disease. My father had listened to my account of the memories from my past life, and he gave it all serious deliberation.

Several years later, after I completely forgot everything I had said to him, I was appointed to this project. Why now of all times?! This work was keeping me from my research! I had been so indignant that I had devoted all my energy to the development of new magical tools that could speed up construction. I wasn't at all sorry.

"The underground sewer system came as a complete surprise to me, too. I suggested the highway project because that's where I can find monsters, though. Well, materials from monsters, to be precise. So I've been hunting monsters under the pretense of surveying."

"Our princess has been doing all that...?" Euphie exclaimed in amazement.

She was staring at me in consternation, and it was quite intense. I couldn't hold her gaze, even though I knew it would seem suspicious.

"No, I mean, the thing is... It's more like I wanted to be allowed to survey the area... I suppose?"

"There's a world of difference between that excuse and your true intentions!"

"Her Highness has run off countless times, leaving behind nothing but a farewell letter," Ilia remarked. "In the end, I said to her that if she was going to go exploring, she should at least do something constructive at the same time, which is how this highway business all started."

That brought back fond memories. I had been so much freer in the past. Indeed, I had settled down in recent years, all because my research was taking shape. My main concern at the moment was to verify my theories and make any corrections!

Any attempt to leave the royal palace now would result in a heated chase from the knights of the Royal Guard and the newly formed corps of warrior maidens. From what I could tell, the Royal Guard treated me as target practice in their exercises.

"Well, that went longer than I anticipated. Let's call it a day for our first lesson. Make sure you don't forget anything!"

"Yes, I understand," Euphie responded with a soft chuckle.

Only when I stared back at her did she seem to realize she had just laughed, quickly covering her mouth and returning to her usual expressionless countenance.

That gesture was so amusing that I barely suppressed a laugh myself. Euphie glared back at me, but that only made me chuckle even harder.

If she was slowly getting used to life here, I could hardly ask for anything more.

CHAPTER 4
Like Picturing a Rainbow

A few days had passed since we had started to share ideas through our makeshift lessons.

By now, we had firmly established the format of these magicology lessons—I was the teacher, and Ilia was my assistant. Heh-heh, I was actually enjoying this!

"So today we're going to build a working magical tool!"

"Oh? Are they really that easy to make?"

"I've brought a simple one. See, one of those Thermal Pots you've been using so much!"

Ta-daa! With a dramatic flourish, I placed the unassembled parts in front of Euphie, who stared down at them with great interest.

"It isn't all that difficult to put together," I said, taking the parts in my hands. "But it does require a certain level of technique."

"Technique?"

"Indeed. I've got a question for *you* now. What do you need to do to make a detailed mental image whenever you use magic?"

"…Chanting?"

"Correct! Or more precisely, conveying to the spirit what you want it to do."

That was something Euphie herself had described in one of our previous classes. Of course, she was fully aware of the necessity of creating mental images.

"This part of the magical tool is extremely important. This is where your crafting technique comes in."

"...It isn't as easy as I hoped, is it?"

"It's all about the process. It isn't all that difficult to assemble, and the basic principles are fairly simple. Why don't we give it a go?"

I showed Euphie the base, which would provide the Thermal Pot's core function of generating heat, and urged her to pay attention as I pointed to the base.

"By placing a fire stone here, we'll be able to make it generate heat. This is where the chanting technique comes in."

"A chanting technique...?" Euphie echoed, tilting her head to one side in curiosity.

"The magical tool isn't going to speak or anything like that," I said with a smirk. "See? Take a look inside the base."

"...Is that an engraving? Ah, that's the incantation?"

"Something like that. So how exactly does a Thermal Pot work? How do you get it to do what you want? This is basically a circuit to provide that core function," I said, tracing the engraved letters on the base while Euphie watched on in admiration.

In the world of my past life, this might have been considered a program of sorts that served to activate the magical tool.

"If you pass fire-type magical energy through these letters, you can activate it even without the fire stone. But not everyone has an aptitude for fire magic, so it's better to use the spirit stone."

"You can do all that just by carving the words into it...?"

"That's why I said it requires specific techniques. For example, applying a special paint containing ground-up spirit stones to the engraved letters. Also, the base itself is an alloy with spirit stones in it, too. You know the spirit stones with no attributes? They're only really used for decoration, right?"

"They are...? Well, I suppose they don't have many practical applications, but since spirit stones do have such a long history, aren't they used in ceremonies and the like...?"

"That's what I mean. Decoration."

Euphie breathed a deep sigh.

No, I understood where she was coming from. People in our society held immense gratitude and reverence for spirit stones. That applied even to those stones that possessed no functional attributes.

However, since such spirit stones contained only raw magical energy, there was some doubt about how to make use of them. They were often ground up and sprinkled through the air in a powdery form in ceremonies and festivals and the like.

They were used occasionally in medicine, too. If you poured magical power into such a stone and processed it into powder, the end result was a restorative medicine capable of replenishing magical energy. That said, the taste alone was practically lethal. I had tried such a concoction once myself, and I had no intention of ever doing so again.

Aside from that, non-elemental spirit stones were still largely a mystery. Were they the remains of spirits that had crystalized before they could develop notable attributes? Or had they lost their original attributes due to overuse?

That was an enticing question for future research, but I had put off investigating it in depth, as my priority was to make magical tools I could actually use. Perhaps I would have time to look into it properly one day.

"Back to the topic at hand; it appears to take a lot of time to process...," Euphie commented.

"It certainly does. But anyone who possesses magical energy can make these tools work. This could lead to new opportunities for craftsmen, new employment, and new ways to make a living."

The Kingdom of Palettia had been blessed with an era of peace and stability. I'd heard the country had been going through a rough patch before my father took the throne, but he had managed to right the ship.

But even if our world was at peace, there was still a divide between the rich and poor. In fact, I was aware of a slum for refugees in the capital itself, and there were untold numbers of poor and destitute subjects who had no means of securing food for tomorrow.

I might not be able to save all of them, but if demand for my magical tools was to increase, the kingdom would need more manpower to satisfy it. I would have liked for my father to help promote the development of magical tools with the power of the state, but there was only so much I could do in my present position. The political struggle regarding who would succeed to the throne was truly a hindrance to my efforts.

That was when I realized Euphie was staring again.

"What's wrong?" I asked.

"...No, I was just thinking how you sounded like true royalty just then."

"I *am* royalty!" I exclaimed.

Not even Ilia could suppress a snort at that, apparently. I glared at her, but she quickly wiped her mouth, trying to pretend nothing had happened. Maybe I should pinch her cheeks...

"A-anyway! There are blacksmiths and craftsmen among the commoners we employ, so why not put their skills to use?"

"Y-yes. That does make sense..."

For some reason, the atmosphere had become rather awkward. I mean, I might not have been perfect, but I *was* still royalty, you know? I couldn't be indifferent to the well-being of the people here.

Who was I making these excuses for anyway? I set about assembling the Thermal Pot with Euphie's help. Getting the parts ready might have been difficult, but the assembly stage was much simpler.

All we had to do was connect the parts in the proper order. The base, which provided the main function of the unit, had to be connected to an exterior container that prevented the heat inside from escaping. Next came the fire-type spirit stone, which had to be inserted into the alcove in the base.

After that, it was important to do a thorough safety check to ensure there were no mistakes in the engraved text. The last step was to pass enough magical energy through the unit to see whether it worked.

"All right. Now we've confirmed it's functioning properly."

"It's surprisingly easy, just putting the pieces together..."

"Creating the parts requires craftsmanship and skill, but after that, even a child could assemble it."

"...I'm convinced. These really are wonderful inventions."

"Do you actually think so?"

"Yes, I do. Completely and utterly sincerely." Euphie flashed me a smile, nodding.

I felt my chest growing warm at this display of emotion. Ah, I was so grateful to her.

Whenever someone praised my magical tools, though, I always got an itch to show them more. If she was so impressed by the Thermal Pot, what would she think about that other device?

"All right! This time I'll introduce my extra-special, secret magical tool that my father authorized!"

"Special? Secret?"

"Hee-hee... Ta-daa! Here it is!"

I shoved my hand down the back of my skirt and held up the *thing* so my protégé could see it.

Euphie stared back in suspicion. "Is that...a sword hilt? It looks a little strange."

It was indeed—in my hand was a bladeless sword hilt.

There was a depression at the base of the hilt, inside of which was a spirit stone. Other than that, the rest was nothing but a regular sword hilt. To all appearances anyway.

"As you can see, it's modeled after the longswords commonly used by our knights."

"Why only the hilt?"

"Why indeed? I'm especially proud of this magical tool. You'll be amazed how useful it is. Behold!"

"E-er...?" Euphie, taken aback by my outpouring of enthusiasm, took my invention in her hands. She looked down at it doubtfully, checking its weight and feeling it in her hands.

Finally, she turned her attention to the spirit stone embedded in the hollow at the base.

"It's a magical tool, isn't it? Do you activate it by passing magical energy through it?"

"Why don't you give it a try?"

"...Very well."

Euphie began to direct her magical energy, slowly and with great care, into the sword hilt. The spirit stone embedded in its base responded with twinkling light. A magic circle appeared on its surface, and more light began to spill from the empty hilt.

That radiant glow quickly grew stronger and firmer, until it composed a shimmering blade of pure light. Euphie was definitely impressed.

"It's a sword, but the blade is made from magical energy. The hilt is much lighter than any regular sword, and the weight of the blade itself can be adjusted to the user's liking! A perfect tool to help a lady defend herself, don't you think?"

"Why do you sound like a merchant now, Lady Anis...?"

Because I was getting caught up in the heat of the moment! Like calling in to take advantage of an infomercial deal! Sure, telephones hadn't been invented in this world yet, but at the rate I was going, it was only a matter of time! Probably!

"This is amazing. It looks like it's about the same length as a standard longsword. But only the hilt has any weight... This *would* be perfect to help women defend themselves, Lady Anis. And it's so easy to carry. Even children ought to be able to use it. Can the magical blade actually cut?"

"Of course it can. That said, I don't exactly recommend it. Getting into a serious battle would put a lot of strain on the spirit stone generating the blade. It's a little vulnerable to physical shock. Oh, and this is just another accidental by-product, but it's very useful for cutting through magic."

Impressed, Euphie held the sword out to confirm how it handled. To the naked eye, it looked just like any other sword, albeit one composed of light. It might not have been well suited to a truly intense duel, and it might not be able to survive repeated impacts, but it wasn't heavy in the hand and didn't cost a fortune to produce. It was one of the few inventions of mine that my father had praised openly.

I had referred to it during its development as a Mana Blade. Several trustworthy ladies-in-waiting in the royal palace had already adopted them for self-defense to see how they worked.

They were extremely easy to carry around; I kept one in a holder attached to my thigh. At that size, they were easy to hide and made for great concealed weapons.

"How strong is it?"

"That depends on the settings. You can adjust the shape and strength to your liking. That said, seeing as it's powered by a spirit stone, overloading the stone inside will break it, and you'll need to replace the stone. Also, the more you demand of it, the more magical energy it will use. I'm currently testing its durability. So! That's the Mana Blade. My father was more impressed by the Mana Shield, actually. Argh!"

"You can make a shield the same way...? That does sound useful."

They *were*, yes, but the Mana Blade was so much more of a classic! As an aside, only my father and Ilia were in possession of Mana Shields in order to keep the technology from leaking out. My father had his as a means of protection, and I had given a second to Ilia as a present.

My father had asked if I could use the same basic principle to create a whole suit of armor, but the settings were almost impossible to get right to cover an entire person. After all, swords and shields didn't need to accommodate for movement. I had tried my best to fashion something resembling armor that could adapt to a moving subject, but it had been too difficult to fine-tune. In the end, I had abandoned the idea.

"You can't use them everywhere, though, seeing as they're vulnerable to heavy attacks. But that doesn't mean they won't come in handy in a pinch. I just don't recommend anything that will damage the spirit stone."

"How much can it take?"

"If you tried to deflect a falling rock around the size of a person, that would probably break it."

"...Have you tried that already, then?" Euphie asked coolly.

I averted my gaze, clearing my throat and trying to deflect. "R-right! There are magic techniques that can summon swords, too, aren't there? Mana Blades are essentially the same idea!"

"...There aren't very many people who can do that, though. Those people usually end up joining one of the chivalric orders. But I've heard people say it's better to just use magic normally..."

"Because they have to do it in an enclosed space or something, right? Well, that's where a Mana Blade will come in handy. Even if you can't use magic, so long as you can channel magical energy, anyone can use them!"

In other words, they were mostly designed for my own use—to be even more specific, I had built them *because* I had wanted to use them. I had always longed to wield a sword of light. After all, I wasn't exactly defenseless, but I *was* a woman, so this kind of tool could prove invaluable. On top of that, they had been popular among the maidservants, so it was clearly one of my more successful inventions.

"So you see, there are ways to put non-elemental spirit stones to proper use."

"I see. By the way, what would happen if you used an elemental spirit stone instead?"

"More trouble than it's worth."

"Oh...?"

"I tried putting a fire stone in one, but the handle got so hot that I burned myself. Water is useless until you can solidify it, but freezing it gave me chilblains. Wind was too difficult to stabilize, and it kept going off accidentally. And as for earth... Well, that basically just turned it into a cudgel..."

Did she think I *didn't* want an elemental sword?! The problem was that it was impossible for someone with no ability to use magic to forge a blade from an elemental spirit stone. After all, as painful as it was to admit, I had no sense for those spells.

The issue was finding the proper configuration and working out how to add elemental properties while maintaining the core function of a sword. Solving those problems had proven to be such a hassle that I had ended up putting off the project.

"But maybe *you* can do it, Euphie? You can add elemental properties through your own magic, rather than relying on spirit stones."

"I see…"

"So I've decided to have a new Mana Blade made specially for you."

"For me?" Euphie stared back wide-eyed.

I flashed her a smile. "Think of it like a welcome gift to celebrate your new job as my assistant. If you have a taste for swords, I'm sure it will come in handy sometime. Especially if you ever have to deal with a surprise attack."

"…Are you sure?"

"It will be custom-made, so you can modify it any way you like! Making these things is basically a hobby of mine, so feel free to get creative!" I exclaimed, taking her hands in my own.

Euphie looked rather flummoxed, but she did respond with an embarrassed nod. "I'll accept your offer, then… And I do have a request." After a moment of troubled thought, she suddenly pulled her hands away from mine and whispered her request into my ear.

My eyes widened in surprise, and I almost burst out cackling like a madwoman. Eventually, I found my self-control and flashed her a grin. "That sounds wonderful, Euphie! I knew you were the right person for the job!"

"…But is it really possible?" she asked nervously.

"I've got a personal rule—*nothing* is impossible until I've tried it!" I said to reassure her.

Caught up in the moment, Euphie gave me a broad smile. Now came the fun part—trial and error! This would be a blast! Mwa-ha-ha!

* * *

When I opened my eyes, I found myself staring up at an unfamiliar ceiling. For a brief moment, I wondered where exactly I was. Then I woke up properly and remembered I had moved into a villa on the grounds of the royal palace.

I shook my head to dispel my lingering drowsiness and let out a deep sigh. I was doing that a lot recently, probably because I hadn't been getting enough sleep over the past few days.

"Good morning, Lady Euphyllia. May I come inside?"

All of a sudden, a voice sounded from outside my door—Ilia, Lady Anis's personal maidservant. She had been attending to me quite a bit lately to help me get used to life here.

I was grateful for her attentiveness, but a sinking sort of ennui had settled in my heart as well. It was like I was somehow gradually losing my bearings.

I couldn't afford to let my exhaustion show, so I took a deep breath to calm my nerves before calling out in response: "I'm here, Ilia. Thank you for waking me. You can come in."

With my permission, Ilia stepped inside and gave me a polite bow. As usual, she helped me get dressed before we went to eat breakfast. Ever since I had arrived here, I had taken to wearing the dresses Lady Anis provided. Her clothes seemed to incorporate elements of a knight's uniform, unlike the clothes I had brought.

Apparently, Lady Anis had designed them herself, seeing as she hated having to wear regular dresses in everyday life. I probably looked a little strange in it, but it wasn't anything to worry about.

It was a generous gift, and Lady Anis had even asked Ilia to tailor them for me. Unlike her, I couldn't bring myself to expose my legs, however, so I'd had the knee-length skirt underneath replaced with a longer one.

Suddenly, I realized I had let my mind wander—when I came back to my senses, I found that I was fully dressed. I rubbed my temples, trying to pull myself together. The next thing I knew, my mind turned to the absent Lady Anis.

"Is Lady Anis about, Ilia…?"

"She leaped out a moment ago. *Incognito*, as she puts it."

"…That's a strange way to describe it, *leaping out, incognito*…"

"She does this all the time," Ilia replied in her usual matter-of-fact voice.

...Right. I hadn't seen Lady Anis much at all lately. She was apparently hard at work on the Mana Blade she was making for me, and she wanted to keep the project secret until it was finished.

While I was happy that Lady Anis was being so thoughtful, I had been left with nothing at all to do. I ate my meals at the appointed times, but apart from that, the remaining hours of the day were free. Given how I had always lived, this was all but unthinkable. To tell the truth, I had no idea what to do with myself.

Not so long ago, I had been all but overwhelmed with my studies and my education to become the future queen. There had been so much to learn. But now that Prince Algard had broken off our engagement, there would be no telling what the future had in store for me until the dust settled.

Now that the situation had reached such an extreme, there was probably little likelihood of our engagement being restored. Prince Algard didn't hold me in his heart anymore. I was rather startled to realize how little that fact wounded me. Perhaps I no longer yearned for the life I thought I had.

But it was excruciating trying to while away the hours. I could feel myself growing more depressed by the day.

"...I wonder if Lady Anis hasn't finished yet...?"

As soon as breakfast was over, leaving me once again with too much time on my hands, her face suddenly came to mind.

What did I even think of her? She seemed bright and cheerful, rather easygoing, and was always thinking about this or that. I considered her a good person, but the way her mind worked—the way she saw the world—was so different from mine. Every time I felt that gulf—whether it was her perspective on magicology or the way she employed and created innovative magical tools—I never knew how to respond.

Why on earth had people taken to calling her *Princess Peculiar*? Why did people dislike her so? Why had she been deemed unworthy as a member of the royal family? Certainly I hadn't had a good impression of her, either, before I had gotten to know her, but now?

She was unpredictable, wild, a troublemaker always pursuing new, unprecedented ideas—that was what I had been led to believe. She was obsessed with her unfathomable inventions and devoted her days to her mysterious research while neglecting her duties as a member of the royal family.

I had heard that she and Prince Algard weren't on good terms, and so I only ever saw her occasionally—and from a distance at that.

Now that I had become her assistant, I had no idea what to make of my life... Nor did I know what to make of her.

Did I find her agreeable? Did I dislike her? I couldn't say. Everything just seemed so distant, so shocking, so difficult to judge. I was sure she was a good person, but still something lay heavy on my mind.

I wished I had an answer for all these unresolved feelings, but my frustration was only increasing now that I was unable even to see her.

"...What on earth should I do?"

Faced with these inexorable thoughts, I made my way out into the courtyard. Perhaps because Lady Anis herself didn't often visit the garden, she didn't seem to have given it much attention. It was a rather bleak sight.

The garden had received only the bare minimum of maintenance, and the deserted scenery tugged at my heart. Somehow, I felt as though I was falling—or as if I had dropped something important.

My feet could have given way directly beneath me. I let out a long sigh. No, I had nothing at all to do. No drive, no obligations. Was this loneliness that I felt or idleness? I didn't know. I just didn't know.

I repeated those words to myself, like a broken toy. It felt as if there were an unfilled hole inside my heart.

This couldn't go on. I clapped my cheeks with my hands, but that didn't make me feel any better. I was about to let out another sigh of annoyance when it happened.

"Ah! Here you are! I've been looking all over for you, Euphie!"

Lady Anis was calling out to me, and I was taken aback when I saw her face. There were dark circles under her eyes, and she was clearly short of sleep.

Her hair was done in the usual way, tied cutely at either side, but even her hair and clothes seemed to droop. It was obvious she had been busy working until this very minute.

And yet her smile was as dazzling as ever. Only then did I notice that she was holding a sword in her hand, shaped like a common rapier.

What was unique about the item was its hilt. The curved guard to protect the back of the hand was finely crafted, and I could see that it was inlaid with six colored spirit stones. This must have been what had consumed all her time and energy.

"Lady Anis, is that...?"

"Hee-hee-hee! Sorry to keep you waiting! Your very own Mana Blade is finally complete, Euphie!" she said proudly, puffing out her chest. With another hearty laugh, she passed me the sword by its hilt. "It's made from an alloy of spirit stones, making it a perfect conductor of magical energy! I fused them all together and embedded the spirit stones into it, but you'll have to try it out for yourself to see how efficient it actually is. If it works, it should help combine elemental attributes into the blade! It should help you use magic normally, too—this is a real luxury item! I've outdone myself this time!"

Overwhelmed by Lady Anis's rapid-fire speech, I glanced down at the sword in my hand. In weight and appearance, it resembled an ordinary rapier. But the moment I wrapped my fingers around it, I knew it wasn't.

From the second I first touched it, it seemed to respond to my magical energy. I remembered having felt something similar to this once before. That time, however, I hadn't been holding a sword. I glanced up at Lady Anis, hoping to confirm my suspicions. "It was just an idea, but to think that it could actually work as a wand..."

A magic wand. A good many nobles held on to such items as an expression of status. They were inlaid with spirit stones that matched one's magical affinities, used to assist in channeling the magic that came naturally to the user.

In and of themselves, magic wands weren't particularly rare. But I had never before seen something that could be used as a sword *and* a magic wand at the same time. The only shape other than a wand that came to mind was a ring, perhaps. I had broached this idea to Lady Anis, but I had never thought she might actually be able to produce it...

"Well, if I'm going to make something, I want to do a good job! Oh, but it isn't complete yet. I still need to add some finishing touches!" Lady Anis said with a satisfied grin.

It was clear she truly enjoyed creating these inventions.

"Right! Euphie! I feel kind of bad asking you to do this right away, but why don't you give it a go? There shouldn't be any problem using magic here in the courtyard!"

"...I suppose not."

"Hold on, I'll get you some protective gloves first!"

"L-Lady Anis?! There's no need to hurry...!"

Nonetheless, Lady Anis rushed back inside. I reached after her, but my hand passed through clean air. I adjusted my grip on the Mana Blade.

A feeling, something close to an echo, seemed to be emanating from the magic sword. It was a strange sensation, as though something inside me was resonating with it. Almost like a pulse. I had never experienced such a thing before.

I was bewildered by this strange new sensation, but at the same time, it quickly grew familiar. It was as if my mind and body were growing separate, but it wasn't unpleasant, and I felt no fear. That mysterious feeling was spreading through me.

"I'm back, Euphie!"

My consciousness was suddenly called back by Lady Anis's excited call. I shook my head to clear my thoughts before staring back at her.

"Lady Anis, this sword..."

"Ah. I designed it myself, but it was a blacksmith I'm on good terms with who actually forged it. What do you think?"

"...It's a good blade."

That was my heartfelt opinion. Even just as a sword, it was a magnificent piece of work, and that strange feeling that had fallen over me when I held it in my hand didn't change that fact.

"I always order sword hilts, so my blacksmith was glad to work on a blade for once!"

"Was that why you went out?"

"Yes. I'll introduce you to them if we get a chance. But first, try it!"

"…Yes, of course."

After putting on the gloves Lady Anis handed me, I picked up the sword once more. Even without touching it directly, that strange sensation continued to reverberate through my body. I wondered what it could be, but no explanation came to mind.

Actually, it felt as though something inside me had managed to gather up those thoughts and bury them deep. My mind was becoming strangely calm.

It isn't unpleasant. In fact, it's rather comfortable…

I closed my eyes, surrendering myself to the mysterious sensation. The resonance intensified inside me, my internal rhythm shifting until it was in perfect sync, and then I opened my eyes.

The sword was adapting itself to me. I directed my magical energy into it and felt it tremble in joy, as though it were a part of me. There was unmistakably a six-colored spirit stone at its core.

"…I'll try using some magic, Lady Anis. Please step back."

"Sure. Ah, there's a target over there, so why don't you aim for that?"

I turned around to see where she was indicating and saw a target for some kind of training. Taking a slow, deep breath, I pointed the tip of the sword in that direction.

When using magic, it was essential to visualize a clear image of your intentions to guide the spirits. The tip of my sword began to shimmer, the magic I had pictured in my mind materializing. From this point on, everything proceeded as I expected.

Prayers, wishes, desires. I offered my magical energy to the spirits, giving them form, and what emerged was a roiling sphere of flames.

"Fireball."

As soon as the image came into focus in my mind, a fireball burst out from the tip of the sword and flew straight into the target, which exploded in flames. Success. I let out a gentle breath, the tension in my body relaxing.

"Whoa. That was amazing. Amazing! How was it?" Lady Anis asked, clapping after watching my fireball hit the target.

Before answering, I looked down at the magic sword. "It's very smooth. It must be one of the best wand mediums I've ever seen. With the workmanship and the spirit stones inside it, I think I have a heightened sense of the spirits around me. It's so easy to visualize the magic I want to use now."

"That's great!" Lady Anis cheered. I worried she might start jumping for joy at any moment.

I lifted a hand, trying to cool her excitement. "Um... Shall we see how it works as a sword now?"

I readied myself in a dueling posture, raised the blade in front of my eyes, and poured my magical energy into it.

Let's start with...water, maybe?

That wasn't because I had just used fire, but rather because I could sense the presence of water spirits responding to my mental image and the energy I was channeling. And sure enough, water began to swell around the blade.

"Here we go. Water Blade!"

"Ooooh! Well done! It's a solid sword!" Lady Anis watched on in excitement, her eyes sparkling.

What looked like a longsword composed entirely of water had suddenly formed along the thin rapier blade.

I couldn't help but let out a chuckle watching Lady Anis get so excited. Even I was astonished by how easily I had managed to apply that magical technique. I waved the sword from side to side so she wouldn't notice my reaction. It seemed sturdy. And after applying the stones, it was only slightly heavier.

"This... This is kind of fun, isn't it?" I said in admiration.

"You're amazing, Euphie! I've never been able to do that!" Lady Anis exclaimed, rushing forward.

"L-Lady Anis!" I yelped, quickly diverting my sword. "Don't leap forward all of a sudden! It's dangerous!"

We had been in such a good mood, but all of a sudden, Lady Anis fell silent and still.

"…Lady Anis?"

What happened? I gently shook her shoulder.

At that moment, her eyes opened wide, and she began to collapse then and there. I quickly dropped my sword to catch her. A cold shiver ran down my spine…until I heard her snoring.

"…Wow."

I was completely taken aback. This was an awkward position, so I laid Lady Anis down on the ground, placing her head on my lap as I stared into her face.

She was beaming with joy—and relief, too.

"…She's so dedicated—so ingenuous. Like a child."

She was older than me, yet most would think she was younger. I could understand, as unpleasant as they were, the many nicknames people had given to her. Even this magical sword she had produced with such ease was a testament to her extraordinary nature.

"…I've never let anyone rest their head on my lap, not even Prince Algard."

…Ah, what was I doing? I had been betrothed to Prince Algard for so long, and yet I had never once thought of doing anything like this with him. I had simply steeled myself to become queen and left my humanity behind in the process.

Perhaps that was why Prince Algard and the others all gave up on me. It was one thing to be betrothed to the future king, but another thing entirely if I couldn't establish a proper relationship with him.

I had made a terrible mistake. But that very failure had brought me here now. I let out a shallow, self-deprecating chuckle.

The fact of my failure would never go away, but this feeling of joy was wonderfully, ticklishly warm. I didn't want to pull away, but when I thought about trying to accept it, I could hardly breathe. My eyes began to grow hot.

"...I envy you, Lady Anis."

And I meant it, truly. Now that I had come to that realization, there could be no escape. Ah... Her brilliance was too warm and comforting, too dazzling.

Plop.

A wet drop landed on her face; only then did I realize I was crying. I traced my finger across her cheek. I didn't want to wake her. I didn't want to do anything to cloud her radiance and warmth.

I didn't want her to see me looking so pitiable when she woke up. I was still unable to grasp the depths of this feeling. All I knew for certain was that I envied her.

Ah, how I wished I could be like her, even if only in some small way.

✱ ✱ ✱

"Ah, I guess my exhaustion caught up to me now that everything's safely wrapped up! Sorry!"

After a short while, Lady Anis awoke and apologized with a cheerful laugh.

I shook my head to show I wasn't bothered. "No, I don't mind. Actually, I should be thanking you for this wonderful sword!"

"Mm-hmm! I had a lot of fun making it, too! Thank *you*!" Lady Anis was radiating pure joy from her whole body.

Suddenly, she rested her chin on her hand, sinking deep into thought. "Speaking of which, we should think of a name for it."

"A name?"

"Yeah. I mean, it isn't really a Mana Blade. Hmm... I wonder what would suit it?" she murmured, crossing her arms as she pondered.

She seemed to be rather set on naming the sword, but to be honest,

I wasn't particularly bothered, so I said nothing and wondered how to proceed.

"Hmm. How about Rainbow...? No, actually, yes... That's it!"

"What is?"

"I've got it! Let's call it Arc-en-Ciel!"

"...Arc-en-Ciel? Yes, that does mean *rainbow*, doesn't it?"

"Exactly! You have so many magical aptitudes, Euphie! You can use so many different types of elemental magic! All those colors make you think of a rainbow, don't you agree? It's perfect!"

So I was like those colors of a rainbow? Hearing her put it that way, I couldn't help but stare back at her. Rainbows were bridges of light, brilliant arcs in the sky. Imagining those fantastic, beautiful phenomena only made me feel worse.

Isn't that...? Well, isn't it a little much for someone like me?

I wasn't nearly as impressive as a rainbow. In fact, I considered myself rather dull. Yet Lady Anis seemed to like it, so perhaps I should accept it for her sake?

I gave her a faint smile. "Thank you, Lady Anis. It's a wonderful name."

Her eyes widened, and she stared back with such intensity I feared she would bore a hole into me.

I was confounded by the sudden attention. Yet she didn't say anything. Just when I was starting to wonder whether something was the matter, Ilia appeared from within the villa.

"Please come back inside, Your Highness. We need to fix your appearance. You're so untidy."

"Sorry, sorry. I got distracted," Lady Anis said with a grin.

"As you so often do," Ilia responded, her own lips curling in a faint smile.

I could sense deep affection and trust between these two.

...All at once, my heart began to beat with a painful rhythm. I placed my hand on my chest, startled by this sudden sensation. What on earth was this? I had never before felt anything like it.

"Lady Euphyllia?"

I glanced up as someone placed a hand on my shoulder. It was Ilia, who was peering into my face sternly. Wondering just what had happened, I stared back.

"Huh? Euphie? Are you not feeling well?"

"Hmm? L-Lady Anis…?"

"Here, let me check," she called out worriedly as she placed her hand on my forehead.

I didn't think I was unwell, but she placed both hands on my cheeks and pressed her forehead against mine.

At first, I couldn't help but wonder what was going on. I understood that she was checking my temperature, but I was taken aback by Lady Anis's sudden proximity, and I froze.

"Yeah, you *are* a little hot! Ilia, she might have a cold!" Lady Anis cried out in a panic, quickly pulling back.

"That won't do." Ilia nodded back.

Huh? I *didn't* have a cold, though…

"Euphie, let's take you back to your room! Come on, you need to get some rest!"

"U-um, you two? I'm fine, really…"

"Ilia, look after the Arc-en-Ciel! I'll take Euphie to her bed!"

My faint protests went unheeded as Lady Anis took the Arc-en-Ciel from my hands and lifted me into the air.

Ah! It was just like when she had removed me from that incident with Prince Algard. I immediately gave up. I had learned it was useless to resist when she did this.

And so Lady Anis took me in her arms and whisked me away. When we arrived back at my room, she quickly made me change into my nightwear, then tossed me unceremoniously onto the bed.

"Did you spend too much time out in the wind? No, maybe this is my fault. I shouldn't have rested on you for so long. I'm sorry…"

"N-not at all. It isn't that big of a deal…"

"It's too late for all that now! Stay put! I'll bring some medicine!"

"L-Lady Anis?!"

I could only watch in a daze as Lady Anis dashed off like a gust of wind. She seemed incredibly worried, and so I simply pulled my blanket up to my mouth, trying to hide my embarrassment for distressing her so.

"...What am I doing?" I muttered to myself, the feeling of emptiness that had been lapping against me since morning striking again with full force.

If I closed my eyes, they would be so heavy I wouldn't be able to open them again.

Just how long did I remain that way? I snapped awake to the sound of the door opening, and Lady Anis charged back inside.

"Sorry to keep you waiting, Euphie! Ah, let's take your temperature again first!"

She came over to the side of the bed, kneeling down, leaning over me, and then pressing her forehead against mine once more.

We were so close that we could hear each other breathing. Lady Anis's warmth was so nice that I found myself closing my eyes again. After a short while, she pulled away. She wasn't pleased.

"Hmm. A slight fever, maybe? I just hope it doesn't get any worse. Anyway, you ought to take some medicine. Can you sit up, Euphie?"

"Well, I don't feel *that* bad..."

I began to raise my upper body. Lady Anis offered me a hand, helping me sit up.

She was a diligent caregiver, I thought as I accepted the medicine and tossed it into my mouth.

...Speaking of which, could this be the first time anyone had ever told me to rest and take medicine like this? Up until now, I had always managed these things myself.

After all, as a future queen, I hadn't been able to afford to show any weakness. Not even to family members. It was rather refreshing to have someone else worry about me like this.

Lady Anis brought me a glass of water, so I drank it down with the medicine. After making sure I had taken all of it, she breathed a sigh of relief and began to gently stroke my head.

"Get some rest, Euphie. I know it must be hard to relax, having to adapt to a new environment and all. If you don't feel sick, it's probably just exhaustion. Don't push yourself too hard, all right?"

"I'm sorry to bother you…"

"It's fine, really. You inspired me to make the Arc-en-Ciel! You spurred my creative ambitions! And I really did it this time, if I may be so boastful!" Lady Anis said with a joyful laugh as she put me to bed.

But in proportion to her joy, the weight in my heart only grew heavier.

…Maybe I *was* ill. My mind certainly wasn't relaxed. I had never experienced anything like this before, and I didn't know how to respond to it…

"Euphie."

As I sank deeper into my thoughts, Lady Anis said my name and placed her hand softly over mine. Now that I could feel her warmth directly, I realized that my body temperature was lower than hers.

Just a touch of that warmth made me feel as if I could melt away into that sense of comfort. It was like I was out of balance, unstable, wavering from side to side, but there was nothing I could do to bring my feelings under control.

"…I'm pathetic," I murmured in shame.

Not too long ago, I would never have allowed myself to act so ungracefully in front of others.

Lady Anis gave me a sharp glare and flicked me on the forehead with her finger. I blinked reflexively at the sudden jolt.

"That's enough! You *aren't* pathetic. *I* wasn't as attentive as I should have been. I should have paid more attention to you!"

"But I've made you worry so…"

"Even if you were fine, I would still worry about you."

Those words were like a warm touch. The shock of hearing them was enough for me to lose all sense of who I was. I closed my eyes, turning away to try to keep her from seeing the extent of my confusion.

"You are so clumsy, Euphie."

"...But I *am* good with my hands. A knowledge of embroidery is a must to be a proper lady..."

"That's not what I mean. You're clumsy as a person."

Ugh. Before I knew it, she'd poked me on the cheek.

"It's fine, really, to let someone treat you to a little kindness," she said, her voice filled with tenderness.

Those words rang painfully in my heart. I felt a sudden tightness inside me and raised my hand to my chest.

That pain wasn't unpleasant—but it still hurt. Inescapably so.

What had come over me? Whatever it was, if I got close enough to touch it, I would want to disappear. Even closing my eyes, trying to reject these feelings, they wouldn't go away.

"...Lady Anis?"

"Hmm?"

"...I don't understand myself."

"Hmm."

"...What should I do?"

"Well, whatever you want, I suppose."

"But what if I don't know what I want?"

Lady Anis still held my hand as the disconnected conversation went back and forth. She had told me to do as I pleased, yet I had no idea what I truly wanted anymore.

It would be so much easier if someone could tell me what they wanted, if someone could give me a role to carry out. Please—it hardly mattered who. She was a royal princess; couldn't she instruct me...?

Nonetheless, Lady Anis said my name again in a gentle voice. "...Euphie. If you don't know what you want or what you want to do, then let's take our time and find the answers to those questions together. You can stay here and have fun with me until you figure out the next step. Just keep me company while I indulge myself. Until that day comes, you're free."

Those weren't the words I had been hoping to hear. Rather, they only added to the almost choking sense of pressure building up inside me. I couldn't hope to deny them, nor could I let go of this warmth that had filled me with such distress.

Her hands were warm to the touch and so comfortable. And yet I felt like I was melting away. She shone too brightly for someone like me. She knew so much that I had yet to learn.

Does she...does she really understand what I am looking for?

But in the end, I couldn't voice my question. Before I knew it, I had simply closed my eyes, bathing in her warmth.

* * *

"...Huh?"

When I returned to my senses, I was lying down in a darkened room. It was night, with the sun long since set.

The only light was the faint glow from a magical tool. As my eyes adapted to the dark, I felt my drowsiness subside. I must have fallen asleep. I remembered holding Lady Anis's hand before nodding off, but she was nowhere to be found now.

Nonetheless, her warmth seemed to linger in my hands. I clenched my fists to hold on to it as long as I could.

"...I'm thirsty."

My throat was so dry; I definitely needed water. I grabbed a cup from beside my bed and called on the water spirits to summon a drink for me.

After gulping it all down, I stopped to catch my breath. I was still in a daze, still unable to focus on anything. It was as if I was losing my mind, and yet I felt no urge to do anything about it.

I don't know how long I sat there like that, but before I knew it, the door began to swing quietly open.

I turned around and found Ilia standing in the doorway. Seeing me awake, she nodded and came inside.

"I see you've finished your rest, Lady Euphyllia."

"...How long was I asleep, Ilia?"

"Almost half a day. As Her Highness said, you must have been exhausted. You've just moved to a new environment, but the biggest change is probably in your frame of mind. Please remember to take care of yourself. Princess Anisphia was worried about you."

"...I'll have to thank her. And you too, Ilia."

"I'm honored... Would you like some tea?"

Ilia must have noticed I was holding a cup. I nodded, though it took me a moment, and she began to prepare some hot water using the Thermal Pot in my room. I watched on vaguely, until Ilia glanced back at me.

"Is something the matter?"

"...No, nothing in particular."

"If you would like to talk about something, please do speak up."

"...Huh?"

"Go ahead."

I had no idea what to say. I must have looked rather pathetic just now. Ilia nodded once more. "I see. Your condition looks rather serious."

"...Serious? A condition? Me, you mean?"

"Indeed. You remind me of myself, a long time ago."

"What do you mean...?"

She was trying to tell me something, but I couldn't fathom what.

Meanwhile, Ilia averted her gaze and continued her work. "It isn't easy to live outside your set role, is it?" she said.

"..."

"Aha, I knew it. Yes, yes. I understand."

Her words shocked me to my core. It was painful hearing her put my feelings into words like that. I had never wanted to do anything other than what was required of the role I had been assigned.

"I wonder if it's a hobby of hers, ensnaring people like us?" Ilia sighed—maybe it was anxiety or perhaps just frustration.

"...What *is* your relationship with Lady Anis, Ilia?" I asked.

Ilia did not show any particular emotion to the question, yet she tilted her head to one side. "I wonder. It's hard to put into words. If I had to say, we're lady and servant."

"But for a lady-servant relationship, you're, er…somewhat *irreverent*… At least from what I've seen…"

To be honest, Ilia's attitude toward Lady Anis could have gotten her beheaded. Nonetheless, Lady Anis seemed to forgive those transgressions. Perhaps the relationship between them was one of deep trust.

"Her Highness doesn't like being respected in that way. I would like to honor her, truly. But if I don't show her the right amount of *irreverence*, she'll feel suffocated. So I play along with her."

"…Is that right?"

"Indeed. I hope that answers your question."

"I see…"

Ilia said she wanted to show Lady Anis respect, but Lady Anis herself didn't appreciate such treatment. And so Ilia behaved in the irreverent way she did because *that* was how she showed her respect.

Theirs was certainly a strange relationship. I could see what she had meant when she had called it difficult to explain.

"I used to be a conventional person, too."

"Conventional…?"

"Yes. I never questioned what my parents told me. I always did as instructed. And I didn't fight back when they told me to marry a well-to-do old man who desired me in exchange for his patronage and support."

"…I…didn't know."

What was I supposed to say? Ilia's voice was as casual as could be, as though she were speaking about the weather, but it was a harsh reality she was describing. Was this the right way to talk about this?

"But Princess Anisphia shattered that conventional life of mine. Now I feel like my parents got what they deserved."

"…You're a very unique person, too, Ilia."

"Thank you."

…I hadn't exactly meant that as a compliment, though. I rubbed my forehead, struggling to maintain my footing in this conversation. For a moment, I wondered whether she and I really were similar, but perhaps I was just imagining things. That had to be it.

"The specifics might be different, but that's also why you ought to keep an eye on her, Lady Euphyllia."

"Huh?"

"The difference between you and me is whether we've been loved as a person."

"What do you mean...?"

"What troubles you is the idea of doing more than just playing a role."

"...Troubles...?"

Was I troubled...? Yes, she was right. I was. She had put even my thoughts into easy-to-understand words.

"...Ilia, will you hear me out? I feel like talking a little, too."

"Of course."

"Ever since I was small, I've endeavored not to bring shame to myself as the daughter of a duke, as a future queen. No one ever told me I had to be that way, but I always thought that was what everyone expected."

Ilia continued her work as I explained, preparing the tea leaves along with the Thermal Pot.

"...You said I was troubled, and I suppose it's true. Right now, nothing at all is being asked of me, and it's like I've lost the ground from underneath me..."

"You've come to believe that your worth is in embodying the ideals that people expect of you."

"...I can't deny that," I replied with a weak smile.

At that moment, Ilia finished preparing the tea. The comforting aroma tickled my nose, and so I accepted the saucer and took a sip.

"...I kept pushing on, but maybe I had grown anxious along the way. And now no one expects me to be a future queen or noble daughter or anyone. I don't know what to do...," I whispered.

Ilia said nothing in response. She merely waited in silence.

I took another sip of my tea. It tasted better the second time, as if my tongue had become more accustomed to it.

After a brief pause, Ilia said, "Lady Euphyllia. You're a very discerning person."

"…? I—I am…?"

"You're much less of a handful than a certain troublemaker we both know. I can vouch for that."

"…Huh? Ilia?"

"So please, allow yourself to worry as much as you need to. But be sure to find the solution to those worries for yourself. Not to become the person other people want you to be—to become the person *you* want to be. The princess will help to occupy your time until you find an answer. She will no doubt want to take care of you even after you do."

I glanced up at Ilia's face. She wore her usual calm expression, but the corners of her lips were raised in a faint smile.

Her gaze was warm, but not in the same way as Lady Anis's. I wondered why. No doubt her expression now was fueled by a different kind of fire.

Lady Anis's warmth made me feel like I was melting, like I was about to disappear. Ilia's warmth was gentler, soothing even.

With that realization, the uncertainty that had filled my heart became slightly more well-defined.

"…I still can't quite put it into words, though."

"Yes."

"…But I'm glad I came here."

"I'm pleased to hear it."

With that, our conversation came to an abrupt end. But it felt good to have been able to talk so casually. I couldn't quite grasp it yet, but someday, I wanted to be able to put this feeling into words.

…Ah, thank goodness. It seemed I had found what I wanted to do; relief and joy washed over me. Now I could smile naturally.

"Thank you, Ilia. I need to thank Lady Anis, too. You've both done so much for me."

"Not at all. I'm sure the princess won't mind, either. She's a softhearted one."

I shook my head in amusement. *Softhearted* was one way to describe Lady Anis.

"She is, isn't she...? But maybe you are, too, Ilia?"

"...You jest. I just follow along with whatever she sets her mind to."

"I see... Um, Ilia? Can I ask you about Lady Anis? I want to do something for her, too. I want to know more about her, so I can think of some way of giving back."

"Well, I'll do my best... But how about a refill first?"

Realizing only then that my teacup was empty, I nodded back at her with a smile.

This night spent in each other's company would last a little longer yet.

CHAPTER 5

The Reincarnated Princess Still Yearns for Magic

The Kingdom of Palettia had existed hand in hand with spirits throughout its history. It was said that the realm came into being after the First King entered into a covenant with a great spirit that was revered like a god. That event became a guiding banner for others to befriend spirits as the kingdom's foundation got underway. Even today, this great feat remained the subject of praise and celebration.

It was for that reason that, in the Kingdom of Palettia, spirit stones, gifts from the spirits themselves, were treated with great appreciation and respect. Since antiquity, they had been treasured as tools to help in people's daily lives and presented as offerings at festivals.

To collect such spirit stones, particularly specimens of the highest possible quality, one must venture deep into the wilds—where monsters also live.

Monsters, though closely resembling animals, posed a significant threat to humans. Where the two categories differed was that the former were vicious, magic-wielding creatures, frequently attacking animals, other monsters, and even humans.

Anyone who wanted to collect spirit stones would have to fight for them. Where there were monsters, there were spirit stones—or perhaps where there were spirit stones, there were monsters.

In any event, if one sought to collect spirit stones, they would be required to venture into monster territory, where a battle against such creatures would be all but inevitable. For that reason, the kingdom often dispatched knights to go forth on the hunt and retrieve spirit stones.

However, in times of high demand, additional manpower would be required. On such occasions, all the knights in the kingdom weren't enough to collect sufficient spirit stones to meet those needs.

So adventurers, those who lived for freedom and memorable tales, played an active role in the realm's economy. In the Kingdom of Palettia, adventuring was a nationally licensed profession, supported by the power of the state. Their task—to do anything and everything required of them.

For example, they might be called upon as escorts to protect a caravan of merchants traveling from town to town. Or they might be asked to solve small, trivial issues that a large organization such as the Royal Guard wouldn't get involved in. As a profession, adventuring was closely connected to the people's lives.

The goal of such adventurers was to acquire fame and fortune by defeating these beasts. While the kingdom might lead the way in subduing monsters, large organizations like the Royal Guard were not always quick to action. On such occasions, a fast-moving adventurer might take the initiative.

It wasn't uncommon that information from these adventurers affected the actions of the king. Theirs was a life-threatening profession, but the rewards could be great. Bounties could be considerable, and in some cases, triumphant adventurers might be rewarded with a noble title of their own.

And so adventurers would accept requests to take down monsters in pursuit of honor.

…But not everyone could achieve glory. The world could be brutal at times. Right now, one group of adventurers was about to learn that firsthand.

"Dammit! *Dammit!* I didn't hear anything about *that*! Argh! Dammit all!"

A middle-aged man dressed as a typical adventurer was crying out in frustration.

He was a veteran of the profession. He had never achieved any particularly spectacular successes throughout his career, but it was rare for anyone to still be active at his age. In the eyes of his peers, he was sober and solid.

He had just stepped into a large forest renowned both as one of the kingdom's premier spirit stone sites and as a den for monsters—the Black Forest. The area was in the midst of reclamation and pioneering efforts and, as such, was a popular place for new adventurers to learn the basics of the trade.

The Black Forest took its name from the darkness in the shadows of its towering trees. Rumor had it that the farther one ventured into its depths, the more that sunlight began to seem like a distant memory. No one knew its full extent.

Beyond the forest lay an untouched mountain range, though none had been mad enough to delve that deep. Most adventurers explored only the familiar fringes. That was why it was a popular place for new adventurers to gain experience.

As for our veteran adventurer, he had just begun training a group of newcomers. He was the leader of the band, their educator and supervisor.

His task was to take budding adventurers into the Black Forest to teach them the rules of the profession. It should have been a simple job. At least that was what he had thought—and what his young trainees had assumed, too. But now they were dashing through the dense foliage as fast as their feet could carry them.

Yes, they were being pursued. Their faces were wrought with fear and despair as they pushed farther in.

"L-Leader! Wh-what should we do about *that*?!" cried a shaken novice adventurer, too scared to stop running.

"There's nothing we *can* do! Let's just get out of this forest and report back to the guild and the knights!" the veteran adventurer yelled back at the top of the lungs, trying to hide the tremor in his own voice.

"But surely not even the knights will be able to handle it?!"

The new adventurer was too terrified to even call the thing by name. There was no disguising the dread in his voice.

"With enough fighters, they'll be able to do *something* at least!"

"But—"

"They can't afford to let that thing run wild! Forget about remote villages, it could destroy a whole city!" the veteran adventurer bellowed to his young apprentice. But not even he was without fear. Still, his courage, tempered by long years of experience, and his sense of duty to these novices overcame his dread. He had given his orders and instructed everyone to escape. But that was all he could do.

Grinding his teeth in frustration, the veteran cried out the name of their dreaded pursuer—the name of the looming threat hanging over the Kingdom of Palettia.

"You've got to be kidding me! Not a godsdamned dragon!"

* * *

A few days had passed since I had completed the Arc-en-Ciel for Euphie. Now that I was back to my usual daily routine, I was busying myself with a little exercise.

After allowing my body to relax in the courtyard of the detached palace, I pulled out a Mana Blade and began practicing my swordsmanship, evaluating my movements, and trying to make my mental image of the ideal forms a reality.

One by one, I carefully attempted each of the techniques I had practiced so many times. I had an unfortunate habit of neglecting this training when I got caught up in my research, which was why I tried to make it part of my daily routine. Indeed, I had put it off over the past few days due to my preoccupation with Euphie's Arc-en-Ciel, so I would have to be careful.

While I was practicing, Euphie suddenly appeared in the courtyard. When I spotted the Arc-en-Ciel strapped to her waist, my chest filled with pride.

"Good morning, Lady Anis."

"Ah, Euphie. Morning."

"Are you practicing combat moves?"

"I make this part of my schedule when I'm not busy with my research. I would go mad if I just sat at my desk all day."

"I see. I think it's wonderful." Euphie nodded in agreement, before suddenly tilting her head to one side. "…I don't mean to sound rude, but those are somewhat irregular fighting moves, aren't they?"

"Ah, you mean my swordplay?" I asked.

Euphie nodded again.

"I suppose they are. I learned the basics from the Royal Guard, but that was all. I'm mostly self-taught."

"I was wondering whether you had learned from someone else, too, other than the Royal Guard, maybe…?" Euphie asked, her head still tilted quizzically to one side.

At that moment, Ilia stepped up behind me, carrying a towel and a drink in either hand. As she reached me, she began to wipe down my face. "Her Highness learned the basic forms from the Royal Guard," she said, "but the rest is the result of real-life battle experience."

"Real-life experience…? Ah, you mean while supervising the highway construction project?" Euphie seemed to find that explanation satisfactory.

Ilia, however, shrugged, letting out a sigh. "It's more than just that, though…," she murmured.

Euphie stared back uncertainly. She opened her mouth for a moment as though to ask Ilia what exactly she meant there, but she was interrupted by the unexpected appearance of a carrier pigeon.

I recognized the pigeon, and I was surprised to see it. The next thing I knew, it flew right up to me, perching on my arm. There was a letter tied to its leg.

"Oh dear, what timing. Just what could this be, I wonder?"

"…Who sent it, Lady Anis?"

"Hold on. Let me read what it says. They only send these in emergencies."

"Emergencies…?" Euphie echoed with a frown.

I wanted to say something in response, but I had to check the contents of the letter first. The message was a concise one, but it was sufficient to convey what exactly had happened.

"...Bah! Ha-ha-ha-ha-ha!"

"...Lady Anis?"

Reading the message...I couldn't help but grin. A chortle escaped me, prompting Euphie to glance back at me anxiously. But I couldn't afford to worry about her now.

"Ah, this is *definitely* an emergency! Ilia! I need to get ready to leave immediately!"

"Lady Anis?! Wh-where are you going?!" Euphie demanded, holding me back before I could take off at a run.

I almost lost my balance, what with her grabbing onto my arm like that.

She flashed me an apologetic look, but her expression quickly turned stern. "What on earth is happening? What kind of emergency are we talking about?"

"The carrier pigeon is from the Adventurers Guild, Lady Euphyllia," Ilia answered for me.

"The Adventurers Guild?! Hold on! Why is Lady Anis getting calls for assistance from the Adventurers Guild?!" Euphie demanded in a loud, disconcerted voice.

"Because I'm a registered adventurer, that's why. A high-ranking one at that."

Euphie blinked mutely, so I pulled out my identification tag that I normally kept hidden under my clothes. The tag was decorated with an ornately engraved name—not my real one, of course—in an elaborate design.

All adventurers had a rank that indicated their abilities and status. The guild managed all requests and commissions and delegated them to members depending on their rank.

One's rank as an adventurer was represented by the same metals used in the currency of the Kingdom of Palettia—copper, silver, and gold.

New adventurers started out with a copper ranking and matching name tag, before moving up to silver, while successful and high-ranking individuals were promoted all the way to gold.

Euphie stared at me in disbelief when I pulled out the golden tag of a high-ranking adventurer. I could understand her confusion. She must have been wondering why a princess was in possession of such a thing.

"Why are *you* an adventurer, Your Highness?! And a high-ranking one?!"

"Well, you see… It began when I started advising on the construction site. I needed monster materials. So I registered as an adventurer to raise the funds myself. And I must have been pretty good at it because I kept rising through the ranks, and before I knew it, I reached gold level. My father must have been at his wit's end when I showed him the letter of recognition, too."

"Of course! I can only *imagine* what he must have been thinking!" Euphie cried in a voice so loud I almost wanted to block my ears.

Euphie's reaction just now was so similar to my father's when he had found out. Ah, it was almost nostalgic.

"I'm sorry. I get why you're upset, Euphie. But this isn't the time or place to discuss it."

The request came straight from the Adventurers Guild, delivered by carrier pigeon at that. The same letter had probably been sent to other high-ranking adventurers, as well—to all high-ranking adventurers. Which was to say that the contents were extremely urgent.

"The situation must be serious. My father will probably receive a report on it before long."

"But what on earth has happened?"

"There's a stampede coming. It sounds like a big one, too; it will be a huge commotion."

"A stampede?!" Euphie cried out in alarm.

There wasn't a person alive in the Kingdom of Palettia who didn't recognize the significance of that word.

Stampedes happened when hordes of monsters would attack en masse for one reason or another. Knights and adventurers typically tried to prevent such events from occurring by routinely thinning out their numbers, but that was never 100 percent successful.

"There are two main causes of stampedes. The first is simply having too many monsters in one place. Monsters are always fighting for territory, with weaker ones pushed closer to villages and towns in search of new abodes. The other cause is when a larger monster appears, driving smaller monsters into a panic."

Monsters were, after all, essentially animals. There were only so many places for them to inhabit, which meant they inevitably competed with one another for territory. However, when people got caught up in that scramble, the only option available was to eliminate the problem at its source.

When a stampede took place, the first task on the agenda was to halt the monsters' advance. If it was simply a mass outbreak, that would be a relatively simple matter, but it was a different situation entirely if a larger monster was behind it.

In such cases, it was necessary not only to deal with the stampede but the instigator, too. And that could be a major undertaking.

"This larger one… Do you mean a magicite monster?" Euphie asked.

"Exactly."

The most powerful of all monsters were said to have magic crystals, pieces of magicite, embedded inside their bodies. Monsters came in all different species and types, and magicite monsters were mutated forms of such creatures.

The problem with these beasties was that they could wield unique forms of magic. There were broad trends depending on the type of monster in question, but every now and then a particular creature would appear capable of highly unique magic. That was why they were so dangerous. And the longer such creatures lived, the more powerful the piece of magicite inside them would grow.

That being the case, magicite monsters were often given individual names to ensure that new adventurers didn't make the mistake of confusing them with others. Given the danger involved, it was generally high-ranking adventurers who were called upon to deal with them.

"That's it in a nutshell. So I had better get going."

"Please wait! Argh! Where do I begin?! Why are *you* going?!" Euphie demanded.

I tried to turn away from her, but she held me back by the scruff of my neck. I exhaled deeply before glancing back at her.

Euphie's face was awash in confusion and frustration. "You can't even use magic, can you?! Even if you *are* a high-ranking adventurer, it's too dangerous! I can't let you run off somewhere where you could get hurt, Lady Anis!"

"I mean, I'm not the only high-ranking adventurer who can't use magic..."

Baron Cyan, the father of Allie's sweetheart, was another such case. The baron was a former adventurer who had been awarded his title in honor of his exploits. I thought I had recognized the name Cyan when I crashed the party at the academy, and that was why.

Of course, some adventurers *were* capable of wielding magic. Oftentimes, a second son who had little prospect of inheriting his family name would join the guild's ranks, as would descendants of fallen noblemen or the illegitimate children of others. Such individuals often became high-ranking adventurers, as the ability to wield magic could give them a considerable advantage.

But magic wasn't the only thing that mattered. In my case, I had my magical tools, and I had learned a great many insights from my research, all of which I put to use in my career.

"I understand how you feel, Euphie. And I know you're worried about me. But I still have to go."

"Why?! And you, Ilia! Why aren't *you* trying to stop her?!" Euphie cried out. I'm sure she felt very misunderstood.

Perhaps she had given up on trying to talk me out of this as she appealed to Ilia.

But Ilia only sighed and shook her head. She knew it was no use.

"Unfortunately, she isn't the kind of person who listens to reason. You've realized that by now, I hope?"

"I can't accept that!"

"It *is* a fact that Her Highness is a high-ranking adventurer, and she has experience defeating magicite monsters. She has been doing this too long to stop her now, Lady Euphyllia."

"...! Why doesn't His Majesty stop her?!"

"He just ignores all this! It's true! My father gave up ages ago!"

"Argh! I don't know what to do with you!" Euphie cried out to the heavens.

No, there was a good reason why I couldn't back down here. It didn't matter if she didn't approve; I had to stop this stampede.

"Euphie. I want the magicite."

"...Why that?"

"First, there's no mistaking that the cause of this stampede is a magicite monster. So if I let this opportunity go, I'll lose the opportunity to get my hands on it. So no matter what anyone says, I'm going. I have to."

"...I know it's a great honor to take a piece of magicite, but honor isn't your goal here, is it?" Euphie asked sternly.

That was true. Those who defeated these dangerous foes and retrieved their crystals *were* lauded in the kingdom. But that wasn't what I was after.

"What I need is the magicite itself. That's why I became an adventurer and worked my way up to this rank."

"But what's driving you to do all this...?"

"...I don't have time to go into the details here. I'm going, all right? This is important to me," I said, staring straight into Euphie's tearful eyes.

I wouldn't give this up. No matter how much she protested, I had no intention of stopping now.

After a brief moment, Euphie let out a deep sigh and looked away. "...There's nothing I can say to stop you?"

I responded with a forceful nod and a hard stare until her resistance broke. She exhaled weakly. "...I understand. But at least take me with you. I've accompanied the Royal Guard before, and I do have experience fighting monsters. So please, take me with you."

"Huh?! B-but Duke Grantz left you in my care! How would I explain myself if anything happened to you...?!"

"The same could be said for you. But if you can go without a problem, why not me?"

I groaned. I couldn't argue with that. If I wasn't willing to let her put herself in danger, how could I justify doing so myself, especially as I was the one with the higher social position? Any objection to this arrangement could be thrown back as a reason why *I* shouldn't go. In other words, I couldn't possibly refuse her.

"I'll accompany you as your assistant. So I have the right to know what your real goal is, too, don't I?"

"...Hmph. Well, if you feel that strongly about it."

Now it was my turn to sigh and give up. We couldn't keep going like this; we needed to compromise. And time was of the essence, so my only choice now was to let her tag along.

"But we don't have time to explain everything here. Can we do it on the way? We'll take my Witch's Broom to the source of the trouble."

"...We're going to have to ride *that* again...? No, I understand. I'm ready." Euphie hesitated for a moment when I mentioned the Witch's Broom, but she soon steeled herself and nodded.

It was such a strange cycle of emotions that I had to chuckle.

"In that case, let us strike while the iron is hot! This is going to be a big job!"

"By the way, Lady Anis, did the message say what kind of monster we're dealing with?"

"Of course. That's why the Adventurers Guild was in such a hurry to send out these carrier pigeons. It's a big one this time."

In my past life, the creature would have belonged only to the realm of fantasy. We were dealing with an incredibly powerful foe recognized and feared the world over. Defeating one was the dream of many adventurers and would win them instant fame.

"We're going to slay a dragon."

I might have been in a completely different world, but dragon slaying was still the ultimate honor. And so as Euphie gasped, I only grinned fearlessly.

✻ ✻ ✻

I received the news just as I was coming to the end of the seemingly never-ending pile of official documents on my desk.

The door to my royal office was thrown open with such force that it almost broke clean from its hinges. A pale knight rushed inside to deliver an urgent report.

"A dragon?!" I bellowed, unable to remain calm. "Impossible! Are you saying it flew down from the mountains?! Am I misunderstanding something?!"

"Apologies, Your Majesty! The news just came in from the Adventurers Guild! It's an emergency! They're waiting on your instructions!"

"Ngh...! If it isn't one problem, it's another! Call an emergency meeting in the name of the king! Convene at once!"

Though this report had just given me another headache, it was my job as king to come to a decision. And so I relayed my orders to the knight, watched as he dashed from my office, and rubbed my hand against my gut.

"Argh...! Algard's mess has already given me one migraine—and now a dragon, too?!"

A *dragon*—that word meant danger. They were the pinnacle of everyone's worst fears. Not only were they prodigiously tenacious, their absolute worst trait was that they were capable of flight.

There were very few direct accounts of dragon sightings. For that reason, when they did appear, the danger posed was enough to send shivers running down anyone's spine and make one's hair stand on end. It was no exaggeration to say that the coming of a dragon was an incomparable calamity.

In the entire history of the Kingdom of Palettia, there was neither record nor legend of any dragon attacks. But everyone knew the stories of other kingdoms that had been utterly destroyed by them. That was the magnitude of the situation.

"Calm down. Calm down, dammit...! B-but what are we supposed to *do*...?!"

This was a dragon we were dealing with. It could not only raze our country, but it could fly, too. A defensive line would accomplish nothing if the monster could just pass right overhead.

We might be able to weather it if the dragon let us be, like a dissipating storm, but the stampede posed another problem. After all, monsters existed to hunt and devour their kin.

All of which was to say the dragon would likely see the stampeding monsters as potential prey. And if we killed what it regarded as its own quarry, we would only further enrage it.

"Father. It's Algard. May I come inside?"

"Algard?! I thought you were supposed to be confined to your quarters... Fine, come in! What is it?!"

The voice calling from the other side of the door was a surprise, but I allowed Algard to enter. As he stepped inside, I could read nothing from his face, as though he was consciously suppressing his emotions.

Ever since his announcement the other day, that he was breaking off his engagement with Euphyllia, he had been placed under effective house arrest, and I had tried several times to question him about his motives. But my son had become unfathomable to me. That was perhaps partly my fault for neglecting him to focus on matters of state, but even so, I simply couldn't understand him anymore.

I could say the same for his fool of a sister, too...

I saw her smiling in my mind's eye, nothing like her brother. Anisphia was incomprehensible in the sense that I could never anticipate what she might do next, but Algard was simply an enigma.

It was my son who broke the silence: "Excuse me, Father. I heard that a dragon has appeared."

"...And how exactly did you manage that while confined to your quarters? What do you want from me?" I asked with a sigh.

What Algard said next came as shock. "Please allow me to participate in the fight, Father."

"...What are you talking about?" I frowned at the sudden request.

His expression unwavering, Algard continued. "To put it simply, I seek honor and prestige."

"Honor? Are you telling me you're planning to slay it all by yourself?!"

"Yes. And I would desire a reward if I was to succeed. I'm prepared to risk my life to that end."

Slaying a dragon would indeed bring incredible prestige. So that was it—he desired honor. That clue was enough to tell me what he was up to.

Yet I felt only sorrow and frustration that Algard simply wouldn't comprehend the things that truly mattered. I could imagine precisely what it was that he wanted.

"...Algard. Do you really despise Euphyllia that much? Are you willing to go this far for that baron's daughter? I can't understand you. Couldn't you keep the other girl as a mistress or a concubine, perhaps? *I* may not have a mistress, but no law forbids it. Why are you so stubbornly opposed to Euphyllia?"

What Algard wanted was to break off his engagement—and to do so, he had condemned her in front of a public audience.

The charges, however, seemed to be utterly fabricated. For a time, I had suspected that Algard must have been blindly in love. But I saw nothing in his actions to convince me of that. His heart was not burning with passion but frozen beyond belief.

"There isn't time for me to elaborate on my feelings, Father. I'm not asking you to promise me anything in return," Algard said quietly and calmly. "But I cannot sit here idle—receiving from others and giving nothing, only following the path laid out for me. Is that the kind of ruler this country needs?"

"...What are you trying to say, Algard?"

"If only she had a penchant for magic. If only she had been born a man.

Did you think I wouldn't learn what you've been saying behind my back?"

My gaze fell to the desk. Algard's accusation hurt to hear. My mind was rapidly going through possible interpretations of what he meant. When had he and Anisphia fallen out so decisively?

They had been so good as children, all but inseparable. There had been a time when Anisphia would take Algard out with her, causing all manner of problems for their own amusement. But when she embarked on her pursuit of magicology, everything started to go wrong.

Anisphia might not have had a talent for magic, but she was blessed with an innovative mind and the strength to realize her ideas through action. And that directly connected to Algard's current predicament. Those around him had begun to scorn him for his utter lack of any brilliant talent of his own. And before I could think of a solution to these dilemmas, the two of them had fallen out completely.

And so they went their separate ways, their relationship irreparably broken. Anisphia renounced her right to the throne and settled into her current position as Princess Peculiar, a fool unworthy of her royal name. At least, that was what I suspected had been her intention.

She had done it for her brother's sake, so he could succeed me to the throne. As such, I had endeavored to raise Algard to be an orthodox ruler in her stead. I had always considered it my duty to protect and preserve the country for future generations.

Yet Algard had always been somewhat lacking compared to Anisphia, and so I had approached Grantz to ask that Euphyllia become his future consort and ensure that the kingdom had a stable future. My hope had been to create a peaceful kingdom, to keep the realm unified without encouraging the rise of factions and strife.

For better or worse, Anisphia's activities had meanwhile brought her considerable attention. A great many people despised her for her heretical notion of magicology, but there were a certain number who recognized its value as well.

And so the whispers had begun—that Anisphia possessed something her brother lacked. With that, people began to compare the two.

Regardless, Algard would be the next king. When I ascended to the throne, the kingdom had been in turmoil. Just reflecting on that time filled me with regret. I didn't want my son to suffer the same way.

I had tried to give him everything I could, but there was no telling how he had received it all. Looking back, it was almost shameful. Even now, I couldn't see what I should have done.

But I was still king. I could not turn back, not even before an obstacle of this magnitude.

"Algard. It is true that the prestige of slaying a dragon would guarantee your position. As for what you want... Well, the kingdom requires all the strength it can muster at this present time. I'll ask you again: Are you ready to risk your life?"

"Yes. I'm ready for anything."

"Very well. Then I shall arrange it. I shall permit you to attend the emergency meeting. After that—"

In the midst of my conversation with Algard, another knock sounded from the door. I couldn't hide my annoyance at this third interruption. This was an emergency! What could be the matter now?!

"What is it this time?!" I shouted at whoever was waiting outside.

"Y-Your Majesty! Urgent news! It's about Princess Anisphia!"

My heart sank at the knight's trembling report. I could see in my mind's eye my fool daughter showing off one of her inventions with a broad grin. And that invention was...

"Witnesses report seeing her riding that magical device of hers, with Lady Euphyllia in tow!"

Right, she had gotten herself registered as a high-ranking adventurer at the guild. And if memory served, information of this sort was distributed to all high-ranking adventurers in the event of an emergency.

A shiver ran down my spine as I put the pieces together. I didn't want to think it possible. But I couldn't shake the suspicion gnawing at my insides.

"Where did she fly off to?! Out with it!"

"I-in the direction of the Black Forest!"

"...That damned girl! Aaaaarrrrrgggggghhhhh!" I roared.

My headache was worse than it had ever been now.

* * *

"Achoo! Yep, the wind up here can be pretty chilly, huh? Are you all right, Euphie? You aren't cold?"

"...How can you be so calm, Lady Anis?"

I was used to the wind buffeting me midflight, but Euphie wasn't. Her arms wrapped around my waist were holding on tightly. She had pulled herself close to me, desperate not to fall.

It was strange, feeling her body heat. And not only the heat but her heartbeat, too. Our frigid surroundings made me only all the more aware of her presence. I shook my head, trying to clear my thoughts before I started feeling too weird and self-conscious.

My Witch's Broom could move faster than a horse at full gallop. As Euphie wasn't used to flying yet, we were keeping just a short distance above the ground, just enough to easily pass over any oncoming obstacles.

"Lady Anis, I need to check something," Euphie called as she held on to me from behind.

That sensation was somewhat ticklish, but I had to answer her question. Keeping my eyes fixed ahead of me, I asked: "What is it?"

"It's about how you're trying to collect magicite. That's why you became an adventurer, isn't it?"

My research wasn't approved by the government, so I had to earn enough money to support myself. It wasn't as if I received no funding whatsoever, though—I did receive some remuneration for providing magical tools and the like.

However, the kingdom's treasury was supposed to be used for the benefit of the people. Magical tools might help the public, but my study of magicology was personal. As such, I was unable to conduct my research on a large scale.

"But if you're asking the main reason why I need magicite, that's because it's an essential material for my research."

"You're using magicite in your research? How exactly...?"

"I didn't tell you much because I doubted you would believe me if I did. But all right. To start with, what exactly do you think magicite is?" I responded with a question of my own.

Euphie paused for a moment before answering. "It's...the core part of magicite monsters... Right?"

"That's what most people think. It's often said that the reason magicite monsters are so strong is because the magicite gives them their own unique abilities. But how do these crystals come to be? Where do they originate from? That's why I started researching them, to get to the bottom of that question."

"And you realized something? Is that why you want them?"

"Yes. I discovered that magicite crystals are essentially a variety of spirit stones that have transformed after being inside a monster."

"What...?! Are you saying they're a type of spirit stone?!" Euphie cried right next to my ear, startling me.

Well, that was an expected reaction. I kept flying without allowing myself to get distracted.

"That's right. Magicite crystals are formed when spirits enter a monster's body and are transformed into a special kind of spirit stone. That's why those monsters can wield magic."

"...That's unbelievable..."

"Which is what I said, right? That you wouldn't believe me?"

Spirit stones were considered sacred in this country. Who would be willing to accept that the magicite crystals found in such dangerous monsters could be spirit stones, too, even if they weren't exactly the same? People would dismiss the very notion as utterly absurd. That was why I had revealed the results of this research to only a select few individuals.

"Just as you can channel your magical energy through a spirit stone to activate an elemental effect, a magicite crystal's powers are activated the same way. But magicite and monsters are deeply intertwined. You can't just pass energy through it and expect it to work."

"Then how did you work out how to activate them?" Euphie asked.

That was the crux of the issue. So far, I had explained the general properties of magicite, and it was natural to assume from all this that they couldn't be put to practical use. After all, it wasn't as though many people had tried real-world applications.

"For a magicite crystal to exert an effect, you need to have a medium through which those effects can be conveyed. So I figured out that I could just use myself."

"How...?"

The arms suddenly tightened around my waist, and I gasped a little.

The next moment, Euphie leaned closer still. "Is that even possible...? Is it even *safe*?"

"I've already done some preliminary tests! It's fine, really! Perfectly safe! I did all that quite a while ago, back when I first devised the technology and started working as an adventurer!"

"...How could you take such a risk? I feel sorry for His Majesty. He must have been worried sick..." Euphie sighed with frustration.

I smiled weakly. I knew full well that I had caused my father a lot of undue stress.

"But this is the only way I'll be able to use magic."

"...Lady Anis?" Euphie murmured uneasily.

I wasn't finished. "Basically, a magicite crystal's latent power is the source of a monster's unique magic. It isn't activated by directing one's wishes or prayers to any spirits. For these monsters, magic is an intrinsic property of their very existence. And that's why I want some. I can't use magic by calling on spirits, so a magicite crystal is really my only option."

More than anything, that would serve as proof of who and what I was. I couldn't possibly forget my own origin.

No, no matter how much trouble it caused, I couldn't just let it go.

That idea had been born when I first recalled my past life, grown through my yearning for magic and intensified when I learned I was completely incapable of casting spells.

"...So that's why you want the dragon's magicite crystal?"

"Yes. I mean, it belongs to a *dragon!*"

My voice was brimming with excitement. Euphie didn't seem quite so eager, but I couldn't conceal my enthusiasm. I mean, the very word *dragon* was enough to light a fire in me!

"Dragons aren't just monsters; they're the apex of all living creatures! Of course I want that magicite crystal! The thought of wielding that power with my technology makes it hard to sit still!"

"But what would you want next?" Euphie asked.

The arms wrapped around my waist seemed to be holding on now with a different intensity. The strength was the same, but it felt like she was trying to hold me rather than censure me.

"Your magicology is wonderful. And your tools will greatly improve people's lives. But just the thought of augmenting your skills with a magicite crystal is terrifying. It would be like absorbing the powers of a monster into yourself."

"...Yes. You aren't wrong. I can't deny that."

"...And yet you still want it? What for?"

Becoming a monster would be beyond taboo. What on earth could I hope to achieve through such extreme means? But I already had an answer to that question, a wish that I kept close to my heart.

"Because if I can't use magic the normal way, this is the only choice available to me. I need to make my wish come true."

"And what is your wish?"

"I want to be a mage. I want to make people happy. I don't care if my magic is different from everyone else's. I want the power to stand up to threats, to create tools to improve everyone's lives and make them smile. That's the kind of mage I want to be. I can't just give up on it because I don't have regular magic."

That was it. Ever since I realized who I was, I had been unable to free myself of that yearning for magic. Sometimes it felt like a curse, but I couldn't betray this feeling taking root inside me. After all, it was in my nature.

"I want to know what lies ahead and what I can do. Maybe someone else will follow the same path after me one day. I want to help clear the way for them." That was why. My words were full of all the strength of my prayers and wishes as I continued, "So please, don't try to stop me. Not until I've done something so wrong that I don't know how to take it all back. If that happens, I'm sure you'll be able to help, Euphie. You're a genius, right? And I don't want to become an enemy of my own country, either, you know?"

"...Are you *planning* on becoming an enemy of the kingdom?"

"I don't *want* to, but I don't expect everyone to accept what I'm trying to do, either. You know, it's not like I haven't thought about leaving the realm behind completely."

Magicology was an unorthodox science in the Kingdom of Palettia. In a country that treated spirits as revered friends, many people would not appreciate my efforts to unravel their mysteries and use spirit stones in the construction of magical devices.

I had painful memories. Time and again, I had thought about throwing it all away. This country was too smothering to live in. The more I tried to be myself, the more suffocating it felt. But the reason I had stayed really was quite simple.

"I still love this country full of magic, and my parents accepted me even though I lack magic myself. Then there are all the people I've met during my time as an adventurer. And above all, I love the culture. Magic has always been a part of our history."

I didn't care who disliked me, not even if it was the nobles who could freely use the magic I so longed for. Nothing would erase this feeling. I loved these people.

They could call me a heretic or a madwoman, but I was still a princess of this land. It was only thanks to my royal status that my magicology research had proceeded as far as it had. And so I wanted to contribute back to the country to show my thanks.

"Dragons can fly; that alone makes them a major threat to the people. Not many people in the kingdom are capable of standing up to them. Those individuals are our nation's treasures—but if they go to fight, they could be lost forever. That why I'm going. I can fly, too, and I can face a dragon. My main reason might be a selfish one, but I'm also doing this because it's my responsibility as a member of the royal family."

"...Lady Anis..."

"And besides, the point of magic is to make people smile! I've been saving my own special magic just for a time like this!"

With that, I walked Euphie through my entire thought process. Come to think of it, I had never divulged so much even to Ilia or my father. Why was Euphie the first person I had decided to confide in fully?

Was this just a coincidence, or was there a reason I hadn't yet realized...? But I suppose either way was fine.

Euphie's integrity compelled me to confide in her. I needed to do this because of who *I* was, and I wanted her to understand that.

When I was finished, Euphie leaned her body against mine. We were already pressed up against each other, but this action brought us even closer together. Her arms tightened around my body.

"I always took my magic for granted. I never stopped to think what magic was really for. So to me, you're truly incredible..."

I held my breath for a moment at Euphie's declaration. She was so sincere that I wanted to glance over my shoulder at her.

"I also want to see further ahead, down this road you've chosen to follow."

"Euphie..."

"I'm sure I'll be able to find what I'm missing if I join you on this path. I really do. So just...don't do anything foolish, please. Your wish is a precious thing. But I'm scared it could end up whisking you off to somewhere far away. I'm afraid of losing you."

The warmth of Euphie's arms, and of her heartfelt words, struck all the way down into my core... Ah, right. Perhaps that answered my previous question—it was because of who she was.

I still couldn't articulate this feeling properly. But I was coming close to an answer. I wanted to find it in her, just as she was trying to find her own way forward in me. She was a genius, closer than anyone else to what I had considered the ideal mage. She was perfect, both by embodying what I had always aspired to be and being a young lady, too.

Yet the more I got to know her, the more I realized she was also remarkably clumsy. She needed looking after, too.

Maybe it was because I liked her that I wanted to show her the path I was traveling. It had to be her, because she was already where I wished I could be. And she wanted to see my journey, too. Her words, more than anything else, gave me the strength I needed to keep going.

"Don't worry. I'm not going to die and let it all come to an end here. Euphie! Let's see where this road takes us together! This dragon is just the beginning!"

"...That sounds like it will be another headache, but all right. It *is* so like you. I wonder what it is, this feeling? It's telling me not to stop you. So I won't. I'll accompany you, and I'll stay by your side, as your assistant." Euphie's voice was tinged with laughter.

She sounded so cheerful that I wanted to look over my shoulder. Just listening to her made me irresistibly happy. It was like a tickle building inside me until I let out a giggle, too.

This might sound strange, seeing as we were about to go slay a dragon, but this exchange had provided me with an important sense of resolution. I hoped Euphie felt the same way.

"Let's go, Euphie! We need to increase our speed, so can you do anything with some wind magic?"

"Finally, a task for your assistant... Just don't do anything rash, all right?"

That was easy enough to say, but as ecstatic as I was, I very well could end up overdoing it here. So I thought as I tried to hold in the joy that came rising up from the bottom of my heart.

* * *

The adventurers who had first located the dragon successfully reported the creature's appearance to the guild—which immediately set off a high alert, sending out a flurry of emergency missives.

As the stampede grew closer, tension was building between the knights dispatched to defend the area around the Black Forest and the adventurers gathering in its vicinity. This was to be expected. A stampede alone would have been a crisis, but there was a dragon to contend with as well.

"Hurry up! Evacuate the villagers! Get into formation before the stampede gets here!"

"Hey, watch it! Keep outta the way!"

"Take as much medicine as you can carry! Without it, your life could be forfeit!"

Shouts rang through the air as people rushed to prepare for the coming battle. In the midst of the mayhem, there were some with nowhere else to go, who could do little but shrug their shoulders.

They were the novice adventurers who had just returned from the Black Forest with the terrible news.

"Wh-what should we do now...?"

"What *can* we do...? It's a stampede. There's a *dragon*, dammit."

"All we can do is stay here and fight. That's it, really," said the veteran adventurer evenly. "If we turn tail and run, the stampede will catch up to us from behind, and we'll be finished anyway. We've got a better chance of pulling through this if we join forces with the knights stationed here."

The novices, however, stared back at him in disbelief.

"B-but, Leader! This is a stampede we're talking about! And a dragon! What can *we* do against that?!"

"I understand how you feel. So I don't mind if you join the evacuees. There shouldn't be a problem if you tell everyone you're escorting them."

"...But you aren't going?"

"I know full well that this is a time to fall back," the veteran adventurer responded with a bitter smile, flexing his shoulders in an exaggerated shrug. "We're dealing with a hell of an opponent. But if running is gonna mean dying anyway, I might as well cut loose and live a little. I'm an adventurer with very few spectacular achievements to my name, but maybe I can go out with a bang. I *was* planning to retire after training you lot."

One of the novice adventurers stepped forward, his expression one of confusion and anger. "I thought you said the secret to being a good adventurer was to live a long life! That we shouldn't throw everything away in pursuit of fame or glory! That so long as you don't die, you can keep pulling yourself up to fight again! *You* taught us that, Leader!"

"Yeah, I did. But if we all fall back, we'll be branded as cowards. No matter how hopeless the battle. But if I alone stay, this story will have an inspiring ending," the veteran responded, clapping the outspoken novice on the shoulder and flashing him a grin. He was taking the philosophical view, and the novice appeared to understand this perspective now.

The novice pursed his lips and held back tears.

"And when you do eventually avenge my death, the frustration you're feeling right now will be what drove you to do it. Not a bad story, eh?"

His followers' breath hitched. The fist of the one who had stepped forward a moment ago was shaking—perhaps in regret, perhaps in dread.

Eventually, one of his companions began to sob. "But if we stay here, people will think us fools who didn't know when to retreat! And if we flee, we'll be considered cowards! Either way, this doesn't end well for us!"

"That's what it means to be an adventurer. That's how you live to a ripe old age. If you die, there are no more chances. But so long as you have a chance, you can still put your life on the line. That's why I taught you to value your lives."

"...You're usually yelling all the time, Leader... But not now..."

"Because I want you to see me at my best, here at the end. Adventurers are a vain lot, you see."

There was a fire in the novice adventurer's eyes, but he only bit his lip in chagrin.

Eventually, a guttural roar reached them from somewhere in the distance. The ground trembled as it approached, feeding the group's anxiety. They were filled with such dread that they wanted to pack up and flee then and there.

"This is no time to quiver in fear! If you want to call yourselves adventurers, think—and act!"

"...Tch! So you're back to yelling, after all! Dammit!" cried another novice from the front of the group, tearful and clearly wanting to flee.

The veteran chuckled to himself. If not for this situation, he wouldn't have been so quick to rush to a decision, either.

Just as he was about to speak again, another noise cut him off. This one was nearby and had nothing to do with the stampede.

"We're here! Ah...! We made it!"

That voice, completely out of place in this situation, reached the entire group of adventurers. And it had come from directly above. When the veteran looked up, he laid eyes on two young girls descending from the sky.

"...You've got to be kidding me...," he muttered in astonishment, his surprise tinged with a hint of amusement.

Everyone was staring up at the two girls, both straddling some kind of enchanted broom. He recognized the first one, standing so proudly, at once.

Even the knights busy with their preparations stilled at the sight. The first of the two girls had platinum hair, which meant she had royal blood. Everyone knew exactly who she was.

The veteran adventurer, though at first stunned, began to bellow with deep, resonant laughter: "Bah! Ha-ha-ha! Ha-ha-ha-ha-ha! Ah, I should have known that *you* could reach us from the city in time! Are you insane?! Hey, everyone! See this fool come to join us?! The greatest of all fools!"

The novice adventurers didn't know what to make of the rapid shift from despair to joy in their leader.

But the veteran paid them no heed as he continued, "Whenever a rare monster appears, you can be sure she'll come riding down on the wind!

Our warrior Princess Peculiar, armed with her peculiar devices! Look at that hair of hers; this is our glorious nation's esteemed troublemaker! The Marauder Princess!"

"What?! Since when are people calling me a *marauder*?! How many times do I need to say it? If you want to give me a nickname, at least go with *mad*!" protested the young lady, objecting to the alias people had given her.

She was of royal heritage yet unable to use magic, a troublemaker notorious for her unorthodox personality and behavior—but also treated by the people with respect and affection. She was Her Royal Highness Princess Anisphia Wynn Palettia—and she was exactly what they needed to overcome the oncoming calamity.

* * *

At the end of our flight from the royal palace, what did I find but *someone* using that disgraceful moniker! What exactly had I done to be called a *marauder*?! I might have forgiven them if they had gone with *mad*, or if they had called me the *creator of magical tools* or something similar, but since when had I become a rampaging pillager?!

"Princess Anisphia?! And Lady Euphyllia Magenta, too... What are you both doing here?!" called one of the knights—the group's leader, I guessed from the ornate nature of his suit of armor.

There was a whole spectrum of emotions on his face. As an adventurer, I had joined the knights responsible for protecting the Black Forest before, but I could understand why they would be perplexed by my sudden appearance.

"I'm here because I received an urgent summons for high-ranking adventurers. Oh, this is Euphie by the way, my new assistant."

"I know you're a high-ranking adventurer, but you're a member of our royal family! And this isn't just any stampede!"

"Wouldn't this still be highly irregular even if it *was* an ordinary stampede...?" Euphie murmured behind me.

I chose to ignore that remark. I mean, this stampede was an opportunity to collect an abundance of rare monster materials. With that in mind, I cleared my throat and continued, "You're wasting your time, you know? So what's the situation?"

"...Argh! We're grateful, of course, but your presence is cause for concern, Your Highness! Our knights, along with the adventurers already here, are presently working on establishing a defensive line... That said—"

"Oh, I know. This isn't a regular stampede, and there's a dragon coming up behind it, too. Even if we can hold the stampede back, once the dragon breaks through, everything will descend into chaos."

"...Yes. That would be devastating. At worst, we could be wiped out completely," the commander responded nervously.

I nodded in agreement. The situation didn't look good.

"However, if we do nothing, there's a high probability we'll be overrun by the horde of monsters. The damage *then* will be considerable. And the dragon could just fly right over us and attack a nearby town or village or, at worst, the royal capital itself. So we have to stop it here. Am I right?"

If this were a regular stampede, a defensive line would probably suffice to intercept the oncoming monsters. The problem here was the dragon.

On top of that, monsters had a tendency to prey on other monsters. There were various theories as to why. Did they seek to absorb their prey's innate power, or were they simply territorial? Either way, such battles often proved fierce. And since magicite monsters were particularly strong, they tended to act alone rather than in groups—and often regarded the monsters around them as food.

That was why magicite monsters were often the precipitating factor behind a stampede. This time, however, since the dragon was capable of flight, it could simply soar over any attempts to engage it. On the other hand, if it was to charge into the throng of monsters, the battlefield would become hellish.

But now *I* was here. The only person in this whole kingdom with the power of flight.

"Let me ask *you* something first. Are you serious? Are you even thinking clearly?" the commander asked.

"I've got a lot of questions, too, but rest assured, I'm serious. And I'm perfectly sane. When the dragon comes out, I'll deal with it," I responded.

The commander inhaled sharply, staring back at me. For a brief moment, his brow furrowed as he made some noise deep in his throat.

I had to smile back at him. I was grateful to see he was concerned about my safety, but this was no time to worry about that.

"I'll make this easier for you. As the princess of the Kingdom of Palettia, I hereby order you to hold back the stampede while I deal with the dragon. Ah, I'll be participating in the attack, too, so take that into consideration when it's time to divvy up the spoils, please!"

"...You're incorrigible," Euphie murmured. "If I could use that magical tool, I would go out myself."

"I can't let someone fight in midair without prior experience," I responded.

"It's just as ridiculous to let a royal princess fight a dragon," the commander mumbled.

Euphie nodded in agreement, but I ignored them both. In any event, I had given official orders as the princess, so the knights would have to obey me. Probably.

"Anyway, we don't have much time. I'm going to scout ahead and attack if I have the opportunity, so be ready to support me by the time I get back. When that happens, I'll leave the rest of the stampede to you."

"If that's an order, then I've no choice but to obey. I doubt I would be able to stop you. But I'm guessing you haven't told His Majesty about this, have you?"

"...I—I asked Ilia to let him know," I demurred.

Both Euphie and the commander stared back at me, their gazes piercing.

"But we can hardly let a royal princess ride out in the vanguard... We're dealing with a dragon here. We can't afford to waste our strength..."

"You're just trying to steal my share of the rewards, aren't you?!"

"Ah... I understand..." The commander nodded, his expression unreadable.

Stampedes like this didn't exactly happen every day! Well, it would be a serious problem if they did, so that was probably a good thing. That said, this was a rare opportunity to collect all kinds of potentially valuable materials! After all, adventuring wasn't my main line of work.

"All right, then. Will Lady Euphyllia be accompanying you...?" the commander asked.

"That's my intention," Euphie answered.

"...Do you need an escort?" he asked, turning back to me.

"Only if you have someone who won't get in our way?"

"Ha-ha-ha, I was kidding... Very well. So the answer is no," the commander murmured with a resigned sigh.

I wasn't a high-ranking adventurer for nothing. In fact, I was among the kingdom's finest, if I could say so myself.

As an aside, even if I was fighting a noble who could use magic, I was confident I could win a duel. In fact, most such nobles tended to keep to the rearguard in battles, wielding magic from a distance. Some of them had learned the sword as a matter of etiquette, but unless they hoped to become a knight in their own right, they would be no match for me up close.

In a sense, I was a natural enemy of mages. An inadvertent side effect of my Mana Blade meant it could cut through any magical technique hurled my way. It might not be so strong against physical attacks, but it really was effective against magic. That thought brought to mind a fond memory, of a contest a long time ago against a magic-wielding high-ranking adventurer. He'd had some choice words after our encounter.

"Rather, *I'll* be Euphie's escort. Euphie, if we can move to a safe distance away from everyone else, you'll be able to annihilate the monsters with some large-scale magic, right?"

"...I'll do my best. At least, I promise not to dishonor my family name."

"All right, then. In that case, *no* escort is the better option. Euphie and I will lure the monsters. And Euphie will destroy them with her magic."

"Yes."

"Then, once the dragon arrives, we'll fall back and change places. How about you support me from a distance when that happens, Euphie?"

"...Are you going to fight it alone?"

"It'll be an aerial battle. You can still offer magical support, though, right?"

Euphie frowned at this suggestion.

This world still had no concept of aerial warfare. No doubt, she wouldn't be able to live with herself if she accidentally hit me from afar. In that case, maybe it would be a better use of her talents to annihilate the stampede?

"Once the stampede is dealt with, the dragon might back off. It's all about efficiency. Do you see what I mean, Euphie?"

"...Even if I do, I don't *want* to go along with it."

"I know, I know. And I don't want to make you worry. So believe me when I say it will be fine," I said, placing a hand on her shoulder.

"...I trust you, Lady Anis."

Euphie took my hands in her own and placed her forehead against mine, as though in prayer. We remained that way for a short moment, until I could make out the sound of the stampede approaching from afar.

"Shall we go, Lady Anis?"

"Yes. I can't wait to see your abilities!"

I still didn't know the full extent of Euphie's powers, so to be honest, I was looking forward to seeing her let loose.

"Stay safe, you two. I wish you good fortune," the commander said, his face unreadable as he gave us both a formal salute.

"You too, Commander. It would be difficult to come back to the Black Forest without you here! Let's have tea again sometime!"

With that response, Euphie and I took off.

Between the Black Forest and the defensive line that the knights and adventurers were forming was a wide plain, divided by a road leading into the woods. At that moment, the horde was spilling out from among the trees. It wouldn't be long before the roiling mass lunged forward in attack.

"There's so many of them... I would be jumping for joy if this were a normal stampede!"

"What kind of princess *enjoys* a stampede...?" Euphie sighed.

"A *peculiar* princess, that's who. Now, then..." I reached into my pocket for a small portable bottle filled with round pills.

Euphie frowned when she saw it. "...What is that, Lady Anis?"

"Another product of my research. Unlike my magical tools, I doubt I can make this one public. It's a medicine made from a mix of powdered spirit stones—I call it *ether*."

Basically, it was like a different sort of medicine that I remembered from my past life. It had taken an awful lot of trial and error to perfect it.

That said, the technology was dangerous, and it would be irresponsible to distribute it freely throughout the wider world.

"A medicine made from spirit stones?!"

"Yeah. There's a bunch of other things in it, too. It took me a few years to perfect it, because overdosing can have pretty negative side effects."

"...We're going to need to talk more about this later." Euphie's glare was as sharp as a monster's.

I brushed that aside, shrugging as I threw one of the pills into my mouth.

"Ah, right. It does have a small side effect, but don't worry."

"Are you sure this won't hurt you?!"

"I'm fine, really. It's just a little stimulating, like removing the shackles of your reason. That's all."

"That doesn't sound good at all!"

Despite Euphie's protest, I crushed the pill with my back teeth. The taste was disgusting, frankly, but I forced myself to swallow it down.

It didn't take long for the ether to start having an effect. For a moment, it felt like the whole world was spinning around me—and the next thing I knew, I was experiencing utter euphoria.

"...Heh! Heh-heh-heh! Ha-ha-ha-ha!"

Ah, this was going to be fun! It was time to go hunting. I would be lying if I said I wasn't looking forward to this—I mean, I had never hunted a monster as large as this one before. I couldn't help but laugh out loud. My lips twisted in excitement; my whole body felt as though it were on fire.

The effects of the ether spread though my body. It was the same principle as the magic that knights used to strengthen their bodies before a fight. However, this carefully prepared concoction went beyond the effects of ordinary magic, enabling me to move like a monster myself.

"Lady Anis…" Euphie was clearly worried about me.

I waved my hand to reassure her. "It's fine! Really, it is! Anyway, it's time to go hunt them down! Give me a signal if you're gonna use magic! Here goes!"

I charged ahead, readying my Mana Blade in my hands—just as the monsters at the forefront of the stampede appeared before me.

"Bwa-ha-ha-ha-ha! They're here! Let's do this…! Take thiiiiis!"

I braced my legs and then rushed forward, pouring my magical energy into my Mana Blade. The horde of monsters rose up to meet me.

Some of them resembled wolves; others, monkeys; and others, what could only be described as large, walking flowers. These would have been fables in my past life, but here they were pouring out in a seething mass of different species.

They snarled as they readied to meet my attack—but it was too late.

"One!"

I began by slicing off the head of the wolf monster that jumped out at me. Next, I used the Mana Blade to stab a monkey-like creature that tried to lash out at me from behind.

"Two!"

With the follow-through, I carved a circle within the horde of monsters, using my Mana Blade to rend a flower-shaped creature from root to head. This was a slaughter, and I was quickly drenched in blood.

"Three, four, five, six, seven, eight, nine, and ten!"

With my perceptions enhanced by the magical ether, the world moved as though in slow motion. There was nothing to stop me from striking out at the approaching monsters' throats, splitting their bodies in two, or sometimes breaking their necks with a good kick.

My voice resounded with raw delight as I carved through the unending horde. I couldn't stop laughing. The materials retrieved from these carcasses would serve me well in my research.

"Gray wolves, killer apes, mandrakes! And a cockatrice! This is awesome! I love the Black Forest!"

My mood had reached ecstatic heights. I couldn't retreat from this stampede now!

But it wasn't long before another monster—a large bipedal hairy troll—ruined everything. It was making its way toward me, swinging in its hands a club that looked like it was made from a carved tree. And it was trampling the monsters I had already slain underfoot.

"...Hey."

My euphoric high was ruined. I glared at the troll, my hushed voice seething with rage. What did that *thing* think it was doing?

"You're spoiling my materials!"

This troll was in the way, and I needed to clear the obstruction immediately. The second it got near, I would annihilate it in one fell swoop.

I poured my magical energy into my Mana Blade, transforming it and boosting its intensity until it was longer than I stood tall. Then I spun around, holding my weapon out like the sail of a windmill.

My attack sliced the troll, and the club in its hands, clean in half—along with a swarm of other monsters that tried to follow in its wake.

"Drop dead!"

Anyone who thought they could stomp all over my research materials had signed their own death warrant. Before I knew it, my immediate surroundings were littered with corpses. Still, this was just a fraction of the total stampede. Meanwhile, the remaining monsters had begun to fall back, clearly too fearful to approach.

"Argh! If you keep huddling up like that, you're going to ruin my materials!" I cried out in indignation, taking a step toward the wary monsters.

At that moment—

"Lady Anis! Please step back!"

Euphie's voice cooled my fevered emotions.

That was her signal. I leaped backward as fast as I could. Glancing around, I saw her land nimbly on the ground nearby.

There was no mistaking the intensity of her magical power. It was as though the whole world was shaking. Light—perhaps a spirit—was dancing around her, drawing a magical circle through the air in anticipation of whatever magic she was about to cast.

"Here create your fiery cage around our battlefield, leave our foes as naught but ash and ember…," Euphie intoned, her majestic voice resounding with the dignity and grace of a ruler.

Hold on, a magical incantation?! She normally didn't need to say anything when she used magic, so what would happen when she boosted whatever mental image she was visualizing with even more power?!

"…Explosion."

With that, the magic took shape—a fiery cage, just as she had said. The scorching heat raged through the massed monsters in a wide half circle, the wind alone hot enough to scorch their flesh. As she held the Arc-en-Ciel and surveyed the flaming destruction, her expression was chillingly expressionless.

I—I was completely enthralled. My heart seemed to have skipped a beat. I was aware that this could perhaps be an effect of the ether I had taken. But even if I were entirely lucid, I would probably have fallen in love with her anyway.

Euphie was so expertly manipulating the magic I had always yearned for. She had stolen my heart. It was beautiful to witness.

"…Tch! Euphie! You're going to end up burning all the materials, too! You're reducing them all to ash!"

I had allowed myself to get distracted by Euphie's radiance, but the second I came back to my senses, I started shouting. Perhaps that was when the effects of the magical ether were beginning to wear off.

"Huh?" Euphie's eyes opened wide in surprise, and then she sighed. "…*You're* one to talk…"

"Come on!"

"…We're going to need to have a long discussion about that drug of yours later!"

Why was she so upset? I stared out regretfully at the scorched plain. Ah, but that magic she had just used truly had been incredible. To be honest, it made me wonder about everything I had seen up till now. She was the real thing, a true genius. She had been chosen to reach the realm I had always strived for.

I adored her, and I was lost staring at her for a little while, when a sudden sound dragged me back to reality. It was a distant roar.

"…Lady Anis?" Euphie prompted.

"I know. Let's fall back!" I said with a nod.

We made our way back to the defensive line. Just as a group of knights and adventurers came out to relieve us, *it* appeared in the sky above.

It was huge, much more massive than any single person, and awe-inspiringly majestic. Even from a distance, there could be no doubting what it was. The dragon had finally appeared.

Dragons were often described as enormous lizards, but that was a ridiculous analogy. They were more like the kinds of hulking behemoths that had appeared in monster films in my past life.

Its shape suggested it was capable of standing upright, while its body was graced with a pair of magnificent wings. Its hands were armed with razor-sharp claws, and its fangs were equally vicious. But most of all, the red scales covering its entire body, and the supple horns atop its head, were overwhelmingly beautiful. It was like a living, moving work of art.

"That's the dragon…?!"

Maybe it had been drawn to Euphie's massive spell, or else perhaps it was angry that we had slaughtered its monster prey? Or was it simply territorial? There was no way to tell.

But there was one thing I understood—it was so captivating I couldn't get it out of my head. My heart was pounding with excitement.

"Incredible! It's amazing! They really *do* exist! The world is so full of wonderful things!"

I had seen a lot of monsters during my life. Of course, some of those had been magicite monsters, and there had been numerous breathtaking specimens among them. But none could compare to the grandeur of what I was laying eyes on now.

My whole body was trembling, as though my blood were literally bubbling with exhilaration. And now I would issue my challenge to this peerless lord of the sky.

"Lady Anis..."

Euphie's worried voice pulled me back to my senses.

I flashed her a fearless grin. "I'm fine! But do you see that, Euphie? Did you ever suspect that there could be something so magnificent? Ah, it's like a dream! Dragons are amazing! I wonder what I would be able to accomplish if I could work with that magicite crystal?!"

I wanted to know it all. Everything that there was to know about dragons. Every last grain of information. I wanted to devour that knowledge, to feed on it. To reach further than anyone had before.

"Princess Anisphia!"

"Commander!"

"...I thought you might need this, so here you go."

The band of knights and adventurers were moving to intercept the stampede, but the leader had approached to hand me my Witch's Broom.

I took it and flashed him a grin. "Thanks. I'll take to the skies, then, as planned. Can you look after Euphie?"

"Of course. Once again, good luck." The knight commander still seemed conflicted, despite his well-wishes.

I nodded to Euphie and climbed astride my Witch's Broom, gripping the handle tightly with one hand. In my other, I held firm to my Mana Blade. With this, I was ready to go.

"I'll be back soon, Euphie!"

I couldn't hold back any longer. I poured my magical energy into my Witch's Broom and climbed into the sky like an arrow released from a bow. As I soared toward my target, the dragon continued gliding calmly through the sky unopposed.

It was flying effortlessly, only turning its gaze to me now. It seemed to regard me as an insect buzzing over its shoulder, and I was filled with laughter.

"Hi there! Nice to meet you! Take this!" I called excitedly.

With that, I lashed out with my Mana Blade, still longer than I was tall, trying to take it down in one clean sweep.

But of course, my blade was blocked by the dragon's tough scales. No, that wasn't entirely correct. It wasn't *blocked* so much as it was *caught*.

"Tch! What…is this?!"

I toned down my magical energy to reduce the output of my Mana Blade. Unfortunately, that action also diminished the weapon's use as a blade, and with the blade no longer caught on the dragon's scales, I was being swung around by the remaining centrifugal force.

By the time I managed to regain my balance, I realized the dragon was staring at me.

The next moment, it spun its huge body around in a midair cartwheel as its tail came speeding toward me.

"Tch!"

I poured more magical energy into my Witch's Broom to accelerate out of harm's way, dropping downward to evade the oncoming blow. This time, the dragon came lunging toward me, its jaw open wide. Its mouth was large enough to swallow a person whole and lined with rows of ominous fangs.

"You think you can *eat* me?!"

To evade the reach of those fangs, I had to turn my whole body sideways and shoot out of the way at full speed. The sound of the monster's teeth clashing together was awfully close. If I had been a second slower, it might have been too late.

A shiver coursed down my spine, my lips twitching in a dark grin. Trying to force down the sense of dread building inside me, I made myself shout, "Excellent!"

I spun around in midair to face the dragon, reactivated my Mana Blade, and lashed out head-on.

However this creature had caught my blade last time, it was proving a considerable nuisance. I wasn't even able to deliver a single scratch.

"Take this, then!"

If I wasn't using enough power, I would just have to apply more. I poured yet more magical energy into the weapon, the light emanating from it intensifying in response. Then, all of a sudden, it *slipped*, as though the resistance keeping it at bay had instantly disappeared.

"...Huh?"

The blade had almost slipped out of my hand, and I was forced to readjust my grip. Glancing back at the dragon, I laid eyes on a wide gash tearing through its flesh, with blood seeping out. What had just happened? Had I broken through its hide?

"Gwaaaaauuuuugggggghhhhh!"

The dragon let loose with a roar that shook not only my eardrums but my entire body. Was it bellowing in pain or in rage? The only thing I could tell was that it was now turning on me with all the terrifying fury it could muster.

"So you've finally decided I'm a threat? Good! I'm right here!"

I was apprehensive about getting caught, but I couldn't afford to let its attacks reach me!

Readying my Mana Blade once more, I turned back to the dragon. When I lashed out a second time, the creature reared back to avoid my strike.

"What—?!"

But before I could even finish my question, I was thrown back by a tremendous burst of wind. The dragon was using its wings to push me backward!

"Not...good...!"

I fought to steady myself on my Witch's Broom as the wind buffeted me. My eyes opened wide in alarm as I turned partly around to ride the current of the airstream to a safe distance.

A faint glimmer shone inside the dragon's mouth. It was similar to the light that had engulfed Euphie before she had employed her magical technique earlier. My mind—my whole body—was shouting in alarm. *Run!*

"A-a-aaaaauuuuuggggghhhhh!" I screamed at the top of my lungs, pouring all my magical energy into my Witch's Broom.

For a second, the dragon seemed to swallow the light pooling in its mouth—and then there was a flash. At least, that was what it looked like to me. The burst was accompanied by a shock wave strong enough to scatter the clouds.

What had just happened? I had no idea, but one thing was clear.

"I'm falling…!"

Perhaps that shock wave had impeded my sense of balance and my internal compass, but I had no idea where I was going. When finally I managed to regain control, it felt like something had been shaken out of my body—as though I had been doused in icy water.

Uh-oh… The ether has worn off…!

The effects of the ether only lasted for a limited amount of time. That was by design as a safety precaution, but right now, it could jeopardize everything. The clarity in my mind was gone, and I didn't know what to do in the bewildering series of events, until I saw the ground rapidly approaching.

I'm going to die. No, I need to land or at least soften the impact. Maybe if I charge my Mana Blade and activate it. But do I have enough time?!

I raced to gather my scattered thoughts to try to minimize the damage.

Fortunately, there was no one in the path of my crash landing. I was some distance from the main battlefield. At least I wouldn't have to worry about causing any unintended damage…

"Lady Anis!" someone shouted desperately, interrupting that thought.

At that moment, I blacked out as some force seemed to catch me in its arms.

✱ ✱ ✱

"Lady Euphyllia, please step back! That area attack you used a minute ago won't help us in an all-out melee! If you know any healing magic, we could use some assistance on that front!"

"…I understand. I'll be right there."

After Lady Anis took off toward the dragon, the knight commander asked me to assist with the defense. He was right, of course—the magical attack I had used just before *could* be very effective, but it would be a double-edged sword in this kind of close-quarters battle.

That being the case, I had been entrusted to support the defensive line from the rear with healing magic. Only a small number of people had the necessary skills for healing, so I could understand why I was needed there.

Strictly speaking, it would have made more sense to send me to escort injured fighters to safety. The reason I hadn't been asked to do that was likely because I was the daughter of a duke, and the knights were concerned about my safety.

The stampede seemed to have limited momentum, probably because we had successfully thinned out its numbers earlier, and so casualties were thankfully low. As such, I could afford to turn my attention to the sky.

My eyes almost popped out of my skull when I watched Lady Anis charge headfirst toward the dragon. Her first strike appeared to fail, as she quickly moved to a defensive stance.

With the dragon's counterattack, it became clear that this struggle would endanger Lady Anis's life. Then her Mana Blade began to glow brighter than I had ever seen before as she lashed out again.

The dragon's scales looked to somehow resist her magic-imbued sword. They let out a powerful glow, a shroud of light that enveloped the creature's entire body.

Is that…a magical barrier?

If so, it was the same underlying process used to create a Mana Blade or a Mana Shield. That being said, Lady Anis hadn't had much success creating a full-body suit of armor.

I clenched my fists at the thought that this was possible for dragons, the ultimate monsters. The only way to get through those defenses would be an immensely powerful blow—or else to fight until the creature depleted its magical energy.

But can Lady Anis do that alone…?

It was true she couldn't use magic, but her abilities were above and beyond most everyone else's, as she had demonstrated when she had crushed the stampede earlier. But that knowledge wasn't enough to ease my fears.

And then the moment came. The dragon finally recognized Lady Anis as a threat and began to unleash a powerful burst of wind with its wings.

I had honestly found it hard to believe such a huge creature could remain airborne on those wings, but now I understood. It all made sense if it was using magic to keep itself aloft.

As Lady Anis struggled to stay upright in the storm, the dragon moved in for the kill.

Even I could sense it readying a further magical attack—a wave of energy daunting enough to send a shiver through my whole body. There was no way Lady Anis would be able to survive it. The dragon had her fixed directly within its sights.

"No!" I cried, and at the same moment, a torrent of light burst out toward her.

That light was a wave of pure magical energy—destruction in its rawest form.

The blow was so strong that the air itself shuddered. It was as though the sky were crumbling. While Lady Anis managed to avoid the blow, I watched as she tumbled toward the ground. Luckily, it looked like she wouldn't collide with anyone, but the impact alone could kill her.

She's going to die.

I charged forward in a panic. Even I knew I wouldn't be able to catch up to her from this distance, but still I plowed ahead. My thoughts were captivated by the sight before me.

Watching Lady Anis fall toward the earth, all I could hear was the pounding of my own heart.

My whole sense of being was concentrated on that moment, when something *changed* inside me, and a strange sensation washed over my mind. To use an analogy, it was like all these disparate fragments had come together to form a complete shape. Though I was unable to fully grasp the nature of this feeling, I surrendered myself to it.

Faster, faster than my feet can carry me, to where she's falling—
"Just like she did!"

Kicking myself up from the ground, I began to float up into the air and flew in a straight line, rapidly closing the distance. My heart was beating so hard that I felt like it was going to burst, when I forced myself to dive down and slide below Lady Anis.

"Lady Anis!"

Her body, still under the effects of the physical strengthening technique she had used, landed straight into my arms. I couldn't fully bear the force of the impact, however, and I collapsed onto the ground alongside her.

"Ugh, gah... *Cough, cough!*"

"Lady Anis! Are you all right?!"

"Euphie...? Huh? Did you...catch me...?" Dazed from the shock of the fall, Lady Anis was pressing her hands against her head.

But she soon let out a deep exhale, caught her breath, focused her eyes, and stared back toward the sky. Then she reached into her pocket and pulled out the bottle filled with her ether drugs.

I immediately reached out to grab her hand.

Lady Anis stared back in bewilderment. "Euphie?"

"Are you still going to fight? Alone? You almost died just then!"

My heart had never been so torn open before. I was at the mercy of my impulses, shouting between gasps for air.

"Those drugs have side effects, don't they? But you can't fight without using them! That's all you have! So why do you insist on fighting that monster without using magic?!"

It was the duty of the kingdom's nobility to fight monsters and protect the country.

Having been raised as a noble myself, that belief had been instilled in my very bones. But Lady Anis was different. She couldn't use magic, and so even though she was the daughter of the king himself, she had been alienated and made an outcast.

I couldn't understand what force compelled her to fight a dragon that even nobles would hesitate to approach. Why did she fight when she had no duty or obligation to do so?

"Why do you—?"

"It's simple, really."

Why? Tell me, why?

How can you still smile?

* * *

"Why do you—?"

My senses, dazed from the crash, suddenly cleared. Then Euphie asked me why. The answer came to me immediately—so unshakable that I couldn't help but laugh.

"It's simple, really. Because to me, that's what a magic user does."

I knew how powerful dragons were. Now that the effects of my ether had worn off, I could honestly say I was so terrified that my body wouldn't stop trembling. Even I wondered whether I hadn't lost my mind.

Nonetheless, I wouldn't run away. My heart was screaming out at me not to turn tail and flee.

I wanted to be able to wield magic, to pursue my research, to learn more about it, and to develop more magical devices. I couldn't deny that part of myself. It was the driving force that propelled me forward. But even deeper than that was a heartfelt wish.

A wish that I had held on to dearly since the day I had started becoming the person I was now.

"No one can be happy with that thing around. I can't ignore it. And *that's* why I have to fight it. That's what it means to wield magic to me. In my mind, mages exist to bring smiles to peoples. That's why I'm here. If I ran away now, I wouldn't have the right to call myself a mage."

I knew I was being stubborn, but I refused to give up on my ideals. If I surrendered them now, they would be lost forever.

"Because even *I* have enough magic to fight a dragon!"

Even if I lacked what most people regarded as magic, I was still proud of the magic I called my own.

This wasn't about duty. It wasn't about obligation. I hadn't been dispatched here to carry out a mission. I simply had a wish, a pledge that I had sworn to myself. I would fight for what I wanted to be. Not to serve others, not to risk myself for someone else in the pursuit of glory—because there was something I wanted to see. That was all.

"Smile, Euphie. I'll be fine. I'll do better next time. And didn't you say you wanted to help fulfill my dream? Making wishes come true is what mages do."

I would always pursue magic. I would always try to make people smile. I had never given up on my dream. That was why I had to go. So I shared those thoughts with Euphie before letting go of her hand and preparing to take off once more.

Euphie tightened her grip around me. "I don't understand."

"Euphie."

"But if that's what's keeping me here with you, I want to help protect your dream. So please, let me go with you. I don't want you to die."

There was a certain desperation in Euphie's plea. I couldn't look away from her tears. I could see she was in pain, but still she stared firmly ahead. Her words struck a chord in my heart.

"If you don't go, you won't be you anymore! So please, at least take me with you. I won't get in your way. I want to understand *your* magic. I'm starting to get a feel for flying. I can help you. I can protect you with my magic. I can support you. So please, please... Don't go alone...!"

She took my hands in her own as she pleaded. I could feel the depth of her feelings, her warmth seeping into me, calming my trembling body and allaying my distracted thoughts.

"Don't go alone?"

I wasn't alone. Euphie was the closest thing to the kind of mage I had always admired, and she would be there for me. She had promised to help make my unfinished dream a reality.

She might have been angry, frustrated, even resigned to my recklessness—and she had still forgiven me.

"All right, I won't. Not alone."

"Lady Anis..."

"But I have to stop it. That's why I have to go. And it *would* be pretty grueling by myself. So, Euphie—will you come with me?"

I didn't know what the end goal was, and no one had ever said such a thing to me. I wasn't sure I'd ever hear it again, and I doubted I would ever be able to repay her for it.

But if Euphie was fine with me as I was, I would do this with her. I would take her with me. *So please...say yes.*

"Yes... Yes." She nodded, breaking out into the most beautiful smile I had ever seen. "If that's what you want, I'll stick with you forever."

"...You're exaggerating."

I stood up without help and reached out to take her hand again. "Let's go do something worthy of that confidence. Let's hunt a dragon!"

"Yes!" Euphie answered in a clear voice as she took my hand and rose to her feet.

I took out the bottle of ether. I *was* afraid of the side effects from taking too many in rapid succession, but now wasn't the time to be overly cautious.

Summoning my resolve, I ground two tablets between my teeth and swallowed them down. The effects were immediately uplifting, my whole body buzzing with vitality. But I couldn't afford to let go of the reins of my awareness. Taking a deep breath, I stepped up onto my Witch's Broom and glanced across at Euphie. "Get on!"

Euphie nodded, getting onto the broom behind me, before wrapping her arms around my waist and holding on tightly.

Now that we were ready, I took off into the sky once again.

The dragon was still soaring, as though it had been waiting for me to return. I couldn't read its expression, but the way it was baring its teeth almost looked like an uncanny smile.

"Awfully full of yourself...!"

The ether I had taken had replaced my fear with a surge of fighting spirit. I activated my Mana Blade and charged toward the dragon. My foe, having apparently learned from our last encounter, turned to avoid the blow.

"Lady Anis! The dragon has probably covered its entire body in a magical barrier!"

"Huh? Its entire body? That would mean…"

"It's the same principle as the Mana Blades, theoretically speaking. That's how it blocked your earlier attack. But if you can break through, your strikes should be very effective!"

"So that's what that resistance was last time!"

The dragon knew to be cautious of my Mana Blade. It had made the connection that my weapon could pierce its magical defenses. After all, this sword was made of magic, too!

"Be careful of its wings! It must be using some unique kind of magic to keep itself airborne! The wings are what makes that possible!"

"Like the gust of wind just before! Got it! In that case, let's aim for—"

""*The wings!*"" Euphie and I said simultaneously.

I would have to get closer to it—while avoiding its tail—to perfect my aim and then glide straight into my target.

"Euphie! We need to get closer, but I'm guessing the only way to do that will be to catch it by surprise and then rush in! When I give the signal, can you boost our speed?"

"Yes! Leave it to me!"

"Our lives are in your hands!"

"I entrusted mine to you some time ago!"

Adjusting my grip on the Witch's Broom, I turned my attention back to flying. I would have to try to disable the creature's wings—or at least one of them. I continued to glide through the air, searching for an opening.

The dragon was monitoring us, too, unwilling to turn its back on us. Every time we tried to go around it, it would turn to face us from the front.

"Wind Cutter!"

At that moment, Euphie unleashed a magical attack toward the creature, but the blade of air from the wind spirit wasn't powerful enough to break through the dragon's barrier. It only shattered into a mist of light.

However, it had succeeded in distracting our foe for a brief moment.

"Now!" I cried out at the top of my lungs.

With that signal, Euphie boosted our speed. The momentum was enough to drag my body backward and send blood rushing to my head. Just as my consciousness began to dim slightly, we shot past the dragon's head. As we quickly circled behind its back, I let go of my Witch's Broom.

For a brief moment, before the dragon could turn around to face us, I concentrated my magical energy into my Mana Blade and clasped it with both hands. Then, after raising it overhead, I brought it down.

"This time, it's *your* turn to fall!"

There was a flash of light. It was no exaggeration to say I had poured all my strength into that strike, and my blade wedged itself into the root of the dragon's wing. There was far more resistance than before. Was the dragon concentrating its magical energy into protecting its body?! Or was its barrier naturally stronger around vulnerable areas?!

"I...won't...!"

Cut, cut, cut! I prayed as I poured my magical energy into my Mana Blade—and at that moment, the resistance gave way. My weapon carved effortlessly through, rending the dragon's wing clean from its body.

"*Gwaaaaaauuuuugggggghhhhh?!*"

That shrill roar echoed through the air, and the dragon writhed as it began to plummet toward the ground. Before I could crash into the earth, too, I grabbed ahold of my Witch's Broom with one hand and lowered us to safety. Just as my feet touched the ground, my vision began to flicker as the effects of the ether began to wear off.

"Lady Anis!"

"...I'll be fine."

Euphie caught my unsteady body in a hug. Luckily, she had been holding me during the attack so I wouldn't fall from the Witch's Broom. There was no way I would have been able to carry out that strike using only one hand.

Now that we were on the ground, I let go of the Witch's Broom. I felt like falling to my knees, but I forced myself to focus on the area where the dragon had crashed. It would have been a major hassle if it had landed in the forest, but thankfully it had slammed into the center of the plain.

"If it can't fly anymore, it'll have to fight on the ground…!"

The dragon rose up from the cloud of dust swirling around it, glaring across at us with hatred and loathing in its eyes.

I swallowed hard. It was gathering more light into its gaping maw, readying its breath attack.

"Lady Anis! Run!" Euphie screamed.

I nodded quickly, turning my gaze—but I couldn't move.

"No."

"Huh?"

"Behind us… The battlefield!"

To our rear, the knights and adventurers were still holding the stampede back. While they had some distance, they were clearly within range of the dragon's breath. Even if we managed to evade the attack, *they* would still be wiped out.

A dragon didn't care whether it killed humans or monsters. To such a huge creature, lesser beings were merely prey, and it would have little compunction about reducing them all to dust. So we couldn't fall back.

What should we do?

I repeated those words over and over inside my head, desperately trying to find an answer.

And then that answer came to me so directly that I was startled. I returned the Mana Blade that I had been using to its sheath and retrieved the other one.

"Euphie. Defend them with everything you've got. Don't let its breath attack reach the battlefield. Do whatever it takes."

"What are you going to do, Lady Anis?!"

"I'm gonna cut right through that thing."

That breath attack was magic, too, not physical. Which meant I could probably bisect it with my Mana Blade. The problem was that doing so would require a higher energy output than I had ever used before.

"That's... That's crazy!" Euphie cried out in alarm.

"There's no other way."

"If we hurry out of its path, though..."

"If it releases that breath attack, I'll regret this moment for the rest of my life."

I couldn't fall back. I couldn't look Euphie's way. The dragon could attack at any second.

"Mana Blade, Limit Release."

The limiter normally constrained the Mana Blade's maximum power output, but not anymore. In theory, I could now pour as much magical energy into the weapon as I wanted.

That said, since the Mana Blade was just a tool, there was a limit to how much it could safely channel. The limiter was there to make sure it didn't overload and self-destruct.

But I wouldn't be able to tear through the dragon's breath attack with the limiter in place. Would I exhaust my magical energy before the attack reached me? Would the Mana Blade self-destruct without the limiter to keep it operating within safe parameters? This was a risky bet, to be sure.

"But it's now or never."

I wasn't blessed with magical talent. My every effort had been a gamble with short odds. Those were the only options available to me. No matter how many times I failed, no matter how many times I lost that gamble, I would keep going.

"If these are my only options, I'll pick the one I won't regret later!"

I must have looked like the hero in a gallant tale, fighting a dragon with nothing more than a sword. So I whispered to myself, trying to calm my nerves, even smile. After all, any second now, the dragon's breath could reach me and erase me forever.

"I don't much care to be a princess or a dragon-slaying hero. But there's one thing I won't ever give up. My dream to wield magic and call myself a mage! So I'll transform the impossible into reality!"

I won't apologize, Euphie.

"I understand. Please, when you're ready."

All right.

"Show me. I'll protect you. I'll cover your back."

I know.

"I'm watching!"

Thanks, Euphie.

A searing burst of light coursed toward me. The dragon's breath attack flooded my vision with pure white—and I fought back, bringing my Mana Blade down from overhead.

"Aaaaaa-aaaaaauuuuugggggghhhhh!"

It was like trying to hold back a raging flood with a simple blade. I could see how insane this was. Anyone could.

And yet—this blade was no average sword. It was a magical sword.

It was a weapon that could only be forged in *this* world, something that transcended the logic and reason with which I was familiar. I'd recognized it. I'd pursued it. The infinite possibilities that had flooded my vision from the moment of my awakening.

With magic, not even flight was impossible.

If people had worked out how to fly in a world without magic, how much further could we go in this one?

"The impossible can be *made* possible!"

If I didn't have enough magical energy, I would simply have to pour in more. After all, what exactly *was* magical energy? It stemmed from the soul. I could squeeze more out if needed! I could pour my whole soul into this if necessary!

It felt like something inside me was being stripped off. But I continued to hope, to pray with all my heart that the coursing light wouldn't sweep me away. *Cut through it. Cut. Cut. Cut.* That was all that mattered.

That white light filled my vision for what seemed like an eternity—until all of a sudden, I could see the sky.

The world, my surroundings, began to find their usual colors and shapes again.

Staring across at the dragon standing in front of me, I laid eyes on a straight gash across its torso. Blood began pouring out of it, staining the earth.

Without a sound, the dragon collapsed weakly to its knees. I couldn't believe what I was seeing. I let out a deep breath.

"Hah, hah…"

My throat was burning. My whole body ached. I felt as if my whole existence had been spent. But still, I had to make sure it was all over, and I forced myself to approach the fallen dragon.

I couldn't tell how far I walked. I could only measure the distance between the dragon and me by the number of steps I took across the blood-soaked earth. The monster was lying on the ground, still breathing. Its eyes locked onto me. For some reason, they didn't strike me as hostile.

"Well done, traveler from afar."

A voice echoed inside my head. I stared back at the dragon.

"…Was that you?"

Could dragons speak? Were they intelligent? And what did it mean by *traveler from afar*?

This was so sudden that I couldn't make sense of any of it. I said nothing else.

"Indeed. You're a strange one, traveler. If I am to be defeated by you, it must have been preordained. This is most mysterious, but it's a delight to meet one like you."

"…You can talk…? I don't know what to say… I'm sorry?" I said quietly. I hadn't expected the dragon to address me.

The lids of the dragon's eyes fell, as though it was about to fall asleep.

"Yes, a truly quaint traveler. Why are you apologizing?"

"…I didn't think we could communicate. And I tried to kill you without even giving you a chance."

"That applies to both of us. I choose words now only because I am on the verge of death. You should take pride in it, like the fragments of other lives sustaining you from within."

"…You know about that?"

The dragon was probably referring to the ether drug I had made from powdered magicite. Just how intelligent was this creature if it could understand so much?

"There are few travelers as strange as you…"

"What do you mean, *traveler*? Are you talking about me?"

"Some rare humans are capable of opening new paths through their inner souls. They are a rare breed who occasionally appear in the world to avenge the indiscretions of those like me."

Whatever it was, it sounded incredible. Ah, I could feel the effects of the ether wearing off. My excitement was waning, and the suspicion that I had just done something terrible gnawed at my mind.

The dragon's eyelids began to droop—slowly, ever so slowly. The creature was breathing its last.

"…There's so much more I want to ask you."

"There is no need. Not between the likes of us."

I was sincere, but the dragon refused.

"I know not what you seek, but I can see what lies ahead. You will devour me as you have so many before."

The dragon's fading eyes seemed to soften with mirth. After the way it had spoken to me, that was the only explanation for the expression.

"You will reach it one day. And if you devour me, I will be with you. I offer you a prophecy. You, too, will become a dragon."

I couldn't say anything. My lips trembled. I felt like I should say *something*, but no words came to mind.

"You are indeed a rare traveler. What perverse fate… Perhaps it was necessary that you and I should do battle—and that you should fell me thus. You are the victor; you may do as you will. Use my remains as you please."

"…Don't you hate me?"

"…Gwa-ha-ha-ha! Ha-ha-ha-ha-ha! Hate you? Is that what you want? How amusing! O traveler, devourer of souls! I shall lay my spell upon you— my blessing, and my curse! Not only will you make use of my remains—you shall bear my mark forevermore!"

The words resounding in my mind were imbued with power. It was as though a foreign substance—words or perhaps knowledge—was imprinting itself on my spine, being etched into me in a way I couldn't describe.

At the same time, it felt somehow like a prayer. Why did I feel as though I had been entrusted with something? I wanted to understand more, but there was no time.

"...I am Anisphia Wynn Palettia. I am the one who has slain you, who will devour you."

Just before the dragon passed, I told it my name.

I didn't know how meaningful this was, but I couldn't let this creature die without saying something.

The dragon's eyes seemed to flicker slightly. *"...Palettia? I see! Gwa-ha-ha-ha! So you are of blood beloved by spirits? How ironic that a traveler should hail from such ranks! Ah, Anisphia. You who have defeated me. Accept my mark!"*

The dragon closed its eyes, calmly accepting this outcome, as its words *"...For both our sakes..."* reached me like a distant echo. Once it was gone, I slowly shut my eyes, too.

I offered the great being a silent prayer, vowing to myself to remember the life of this beast. As I did so, I began to feel light-headed, my strength drained from me, and I swayed on my feet.

Just as I began to topple backward, someone caught me in their arms.

"Lady Anis!"

It was Euphie. With her supporting me, I turned around to face her.

"Are you feeling all right?" she asked, her tearful, worried eyes searching me. "You were walking around in a daze, muttering to yourself."

"...Huh? You didn't hear it?"

She really didn't seem to know what I was talking about. So the dragon had spoken only to me. I wished we could have conversed longer. The creature seemed to know so much about things I barely understood. And a lot of what it had said was kind of bothering me...

"...Right! What about the stampede?!"

This was no time to bask in victory. What had happened with the stampede that the dragon had caused? It was one thing to defeat the dragon itself, but we couldn't afford to forget about the other monsters, either.

"The monsters started retreating into the forest the minute the dragon fell... See?" Euphie said with a faint smile, motioning over her shoulder.

If I strained my ears, I could make out what sounded like distant battle cries—although the effort made me feel like collapsing all over again.

"...I see. So everyone behind me is all right. Thank goodness..."

"...You truly were reckless, you know?"

"For once, I can't deny it..."

"...I'm just glad you're unharmed," Euphie said, wrapping her arms tightly around me. Her whole body was trembling.

It would be difficult to do that attack again, and I would prefer not to. And I regretted what I had done. But if I were to find myself in the same situation all over again, I would probably still have fought.

Still, if it would leave Euphie this upset, I might want to try something different next time. I would have to increase the amount of options available to me—and to do that, I needed more tools, more knowledge, more skills at my disposal.

"...I've got a long way to go."

I leaned back into Euphie's arms, feeling my consciousness fading. But there was still something I had to do. I placed a hand on Euphie's shoulder and stood up by myself.

"Lady Anis?"

"...I've been entrusted with something. Something I need to do."

I walked up to the motionless dragon and picked up my Mana Blade. Feeling around with my hands, I searched for a gap in its scales and cut through the flesh.

"...Here it is."

The dragon's magicite crystal was buried deep in its chest. It was like a beautiful jewel, more than enough to serve as a badge of honor. I carefully removed it from its corpse.

"...Look how big it is. What should I do with it?"

I smiled a little at the sight of the oversize magicite crystal.

At that moment, I heard the sound of horses approaching from the distance. The knights were coming our way. Maybe I could ask them to carry me back...?

With that thought, I breathed out a sigh and relaxed. My whole body had been aching for some time, and I was still a bit stunned. When the knights arrived, I would have to ask them to handle everything here...

"...Lady Anis, please take it easy."

"...Sorry, Euphie. I guess I'm a little tired..."

Euphie caught me in a warm hug. Her embrace was soothing, a welcome remedy for my exhausted, overworked body.

Before long, I was drifting into unconsciousness. There was still so much to do—but this time, I was utterly exhausted. It was getting harder and harder to even move my fingers. I just needed to rest a bit. Just a little. Then I could get up.

"...You did well, Lady Anis. Truly."

Before my consciousness faded completely, I thought I heard Euphie's gentle, comforting voice.

ENDING

I really had meant to get up again soon, you know? But I ended up sleeping for three full days after slaying the dragon—that's what happens when you drain too much energy and take too many doses of ether. When I finally came to my senses, I was in my room in the royal villa.

"Good morning, Your Highness."

"…Ilia? Am I…in the royal villa…? What happened to the dragon?!"

"Please calm down. You've been asleep for three days since the battle."

"It's been three days?!"

"His Majesty asked us to send word as soon as you awoke. I believe he will be coming to visit us."

"Oh no."

If I hadn't fallen into this state, I could have probably come up with an excuse to explain everything, but breaking out of the royal palace and coming back bedridden would definitely earn me a lecture! *No, I don't want to see him!*

"I'll call him, then."

"Ilia! Let's talk! Help me convince him…!"

"I'm afraid I can't help there. Miss Euphyllia has already come to an arrangement with His Majesty, so there's nothing more I can do. Hee-hee-hee."

"Don't laugh! Ah, ow! Why does my whole body hurt?!"

"If you'll excuse me. Hee-hee-hee…"

"No! Wait, Ilia! At least give me one more day…!"

But in spite of my desperate pleas, Ilia departed the room with an expressionless face and an eerie laugh. I thought about running away and hiding, but I definitely wasn't in the condition for it. I had no choice but to swallow my tears and accept my fate.

A short time later, my father appeared—and he wasn't alone. Euphie and Duke Grantz were with him, too. At this point, I was about ready to give up. I wanted to flee with all my might. I wanted to spin around and make a break for it right then, but it hurt so much just to turn my head!

"...I see my fool daughter is finally awake."

"Father. I'm so delighted to see you! How are you, if I may ask?!"

"Ha-ha-ha. Can you not see that I am furious?"

Ah, I had suspected as much. I was trying to laugh cheerfully, but the pressure I was under here was immense!

"You blasted fool!"

"Yeep!"

My whole brain recoiled in response to my father's angry voice.

"What kind of royal throws themselves into the front line, let alone tries to rush a dragon?! And what were you thinking, getting Euphyllia involved?!"

"W-well, my reasons are incredibly profound, you see..."

"What?"

"I'm sorry! It was selfish of me! I shouldn't have dragged Euphie into it!" I cried out. My father's presence was like a weight bearing down on me; his anger had practically coalesced into a dense ball of black rage.

But after my apology, my father gradually relented, and the pressure lessened. He let out a deep sigh and rubbed his brow with one hand. "...You truly are a handful. Euphyllia has told me everything. Apparently, if you hadn't leaped into action, the outcome would have been much worse."

"Really?"

"With our normal fighting forces, we would have had no choice but to wait for the dragon to exhaust its magic—or else fight it with enchanted weapons like yours. But there are very few people capable of doing that, and it would have taken some time to prepare them. There's no doubt that your actions have kept the damage to a minimum."

I nodded in agreement. The dragon's entire body had been shrouded in magic, so it must have been incredibly powerful. With regular magic, it would have probably taken repeated strikes with techniques as powerful as Euphie's to get past its defenses.

And fighting it normally would have required constant magical attacks to exhaust its stamina and magic reserves. But that wouldn't stop it from advancing, nor from wreaking immense destruction. So ultimately, jumping out and attacking it head-on had been for the best.

"But you bungling, fool, idiot daughter. You've created a real mess this time!"

"No, I know I acted rather selfishly, but if I helped save lives…"

"Yes, I suppose you do deserve praise for that. But then there's your position to consider. And more importantly, you got in Algard's way."

"Huh? Allie?"

I failed to see what my brother had to do with all this.

"Algard was keen to participate in the battle against the dragon. He was probably trying to make up for the mess he caused, so he wanted to confront the dragon himself."

"…Huh? You're saying I ruined his plan?"

"Utterly."

Uh-oh! I hadn't meant to do that! Wait, hadn't he been confined to his quarters?! Why couldn't he just behave himself for once?! Well, that might sound strange coming from me, but still!

"You've always done whatever you please, without ever considering those around you—but this time, you've gone too far. Why on earth do you always have to go to such extremes?! Thanks to you, Algard is back under house arrest, and you have two completely opposite reputations!"

"You're saying I'm both a selfish, willful, crazy princess and a courageous dragon slayer, too…?"

"I suppose that sums it up." My father breathed a deep sigh.

I was fine with both reputations, but all the same…

"...How much damage did the stampede cause?"

"Casualties were few. There were some serious injuries, but considering that we were dealing with a stampede *and* a dragon, the damage was surprisingly light."

"That's a relief. Saving others is much more important than my own reputation."

I had long ago resigned myself to the fact that I wasn't good enough as a member of the royal family. There were more important things than how other people saw me. First of all, the knights and adventurers hadn't sustained much damage, so that was a relief. And of course, there was one more thing that was important to me.

"And the dragon's materials are mine, right?! I defeated it, after all!"

"I knew that was your real goal, you boneheaded...! Don't you realize how great a treasure they are for the kingdom?!"

"I don't mean everything! At least let me have the magicite crystal! It was bequeathed to me!"

"Huh? What do you mean, *bequeathed*?" My father stared back at me with suspicion.

Euphie, Duke Grantz, and Ilia, too, were all watching me carefully. I winced a little, but I couldn't give up now.

"The dragon entrusted it to me. So please, at least let me have the magicite."

"Hold on, Anis. Hold on. You're saying you *spoke* with the dragon?!"

"Well, more like it spoke *at* me..."

My father exclaimed in astonishment, while Euphie seemed to murmur something under her breath. I could hardly believe it, either, but it had happened, so that was that. And besides, even if the dragon hadn't entrusted the magicite to me, I would still have wanted it.

"I think the dragon only spoke because I defeated it. But it doesn't matter whether you believe me. I'll accept any punishment for my recklessness. But please, just let me have the magicite crystal."

"...Ah... It's always one nuisance after another..."

"...Your Majesty, if I may?"

"...What now, Grantz?"

"I have some ideas regarding how to dispose of the dragon, as well as some ideas about appropriate rewards and punishments for Princess Anisphia."

"...Go on."

"Yes. The princess defeated the dragon; that can't be concealed. And it *is* a fact that she made a significant contribution to the effort. Given the circumstances, punishing her for her actions will be met with great resistance from the common people, while failing to punish her will be considered an affront by the nobility."

"So if we punish her, the commoners will be up in arms, but if we let her go, the nobility will be?" my father said, his brow furrowing in a frown.

Grantz nodded. "It's true that the princess needs to be punished. But how about I shield her from the worst of it? I can say that her recklessness this time was driven by her desire to link her achievements to Euphyllia."

"What are you saying, Father?" Euphie asked in surprise, staring wide-eyed at the duke.

I, too, was taken aback.

"Wouldn't that make it look like I've been supporting the House of Magenta?"

"Indeed, it would. But you must admit, it isn't exactly a lie, is it?"

"I suppose not..."

I had originally invited Euphie to be my assistant to give her a chance to make a name for herself and undo the damage that had been done to her reputation by her failed engagement. And she *had* worked with me to stop a stampede and defeat a dragon. In a way, it was no exaggeration to say I had accomplished what I had set out to do.

"Now that it's already finished, we can't deny that Prince Algard's ambitions have been stymied. The necessity of restoring Euphyllia's honor has put us in direct conflict."

"Is that why you want to shield Anis, Grantz?"

"It is. I'll take the position that I want to thank the royal family—and Princess Anisphia in particular."

"Are you saying you want to bring Princess Anisphia into your faction, Father?" Euphie asked.

"Euphie. We were originally a military faction. A great many of our associates have a favorable view of the princess. Now that we're butting heads with Prince Algard directly, we can't afford to leave her position hanging in the air."

"R-right, but I don't want to get caught up in any political troubles!" I cried out.

"I'm afraid you made too big a scene this time. This is your only option."

"N-no...!"

Nghhhhh! But seeing as I had decided to protect Euphie, I would inevitably have to confront Allie in one way or another. We had been on bad terms for a while, but he had never tried to actively get rid of me so long as I kept out of the limelight.

I had already renounced my claim to the throne, and I had declared that I wouldn't interfere with Allie's succession—but thanks to the ridiculous way he'd broken off his engagement with Euphie, my social standing seemed to be rising.

And now that I had defeated a dragon, it was sure to increase even higher. If people learned I had done all this to help restore Euphie's honor, people would get only more excited. I was fine standing out from the crowd as a troublemaker, but it would be too much trouble to be a regular sort of famous.

"Hmm... I can't say it's a bad plan...," my father murmured.

"Princess Anisphia. Let's say we treat this as a debt."

"A debt?"

"Yes. I'm sure that given this incident and Prince Algard's blunder, there will be more than a few people seeking to curry favor with you. Allow me to handle them."

"...Ah. So I'll have to pay you back someday?"

"This is my way of thanking you for saving Euphie. Although I do have my own agenda as well."

Huh. To be honest, I didn't love political intrigue. I didn't want to get caught up in any conspiracies, so I had been actively keeping a distance from such matters.

But this time, after all that mess, I wouldn't be able to remove myself from this scheme. My father couldn't handle this alone, what with how big the situation had become. And there was no course of action that would satisfy both the people and the nobility at the same time. That being the case, the best option available was to rely on the assistance of an experienced politicker.

Duke Grantz was willing to take on that role. In other words, he would shield me to resolve this affair.

But if I agreed to his proposal, I would be regarded as a member of his faction. I wasn't even at odds with his political allies, and yet...

Duke Grantz was the chancellor of the realm and my father's counselor. At the same time, he was also the head of the Ministry of Defense, the organization responsible for protecting the country and overseeing the chivalric orders active in each region, which was why he had described his faction as a militaristic one.

I myself had worked with the Border Guard during my time as an adventurer, traveling to various locations as part of my missions. I wasn't on bad terms with the Royal Guard, either, and I had received sword lessons from them—even if they had treated me as a bit of an eccentric. All the same, that didn't mean I could read the duke's intentions.

"...Duke Grantz. You aren't going to object to Allie becoming king or anything after the incident with Euphyllia, are you?"

"His conduct *has* called his suitability into question, but that was already partially apparent even before he broke off the betrothal. So long as Prince Algard doesn't turn out to be a fool acting against the interests of the realm, we aren't planning on moving against him."

Hmm... Well, I didn't really have a choice either way. I would prefer to keep my head down, but given the circumstances, a little strife did seem inevitable. It might have been avoidable if we were talking about everyday problems, but we couldn't ignore a dragon. I was sure that that was why Duke Grantz had come out with this proposal. So it was all out of my hands...

"...A debt it is. Can you help me out with this, then?"

"Very well. I assume you have no objections, Your Majesty?"

"...Oh, I don't mind. I'm sure you've been musing about this since we first heard how it all ended, haven't you, Grantz?"

"I only wish to show my loyalty to Your Majesty by acting in the greater interest of the realm," the duke said with a reverent bow.

My father scowled and turned back to me, letting out a deep sigh. "Anis. Your punishment will be to participate in the celebrations as befitting a member of the royal family. From your dress to your behavior, for once, please refrain from anything wild and be as modest as you can."

"Huh?! You mean there's going to be banquet for defeating the dragon?! And you want me to play a leading role?!"

"Obviously, you dolt!" my father cried out. "*You're* the one who did it! So from now on, you had better act like a princess and work a little harder at extinguishing the fires you've started!"

Was he thinking about changing his mind about me being a legitimate princess? I didn't like the sound of that... But I couldn't say anything in protest. Ugh, how I *wished* I could. Why did *I* have to attend the celebrations? And acting like a princess? That would be suffocating! I couldn't possibly do that!

"We should also formally announce that Euphyllia has become an official assistant to Princess Anisphia and tout her role in this achievement. Yes, this will be a good opportunity."

"Ughhhhh! Nooooo! I don't want to be a princess!"

"Don't you go throwing a tantrum now, you daft girl!"

My father could yell at me all he wanted, but I still didn't like it! Argh, I was starting to feel depressed already. I just wanted to get out of there.

"Euphyllia. I'll need you to help teach Anis manners. And make sure she doesn't run off."

"Understood, Your Majesty."

"Arghhhhh, nooooo! I hate lessons in etiquette!"

"There is also going to be a dance. Be sure not to embarrass the royal family."

"Noooooooooo!"

But the others, ignoring my pleas, began to consult with one another. And so I was left behind, steaming with my own resentments. With no one left to complain to, I could only hang my head and give up.

* * *

After the date of the banquet to celebrate that the dragon slaying was set in stone, time flew by at a dizzying pace. As soon as I was feeling better, I had to get my measurements taken for a new dress, and I began reviewing my etiquette and dancing. I hadn't done this since I was a child, and I felt like my head would burst memorizing everything I had neglected.

I lived in fear of Euphie and Ilia, who had been put in charge of my education. Once, I got fed up with all that rote memorization and tried to run away, but the two of them soon caught me. After that, they kept an eye on me at all times, and so I had to give up any ideas of an escape attempt.

Then, in the blink of an eye, the day of the celebration was upon us. I was utterly exhausted even before the event got underway. The dress I had been forced into only made me feel worse. It was so heavy that my shoulders felt dull and stiff.

It was a rush job, but Ilia had been working on it for a while beforehand on the assumption that I would one day need a good dress for formal occasions. As ever, she was a fantastic maid. But I would never forgive her for this. When on earth had she even designed this thing...?

The dress was the perfect attire for a royal princess attending a banquet. If I wasn't the one who had to wear it, I would have readily lauded it as a work of art.

Its soft-pink tones were decorated with white frills, and the patterned embroidery was simply splendid, while the ornate jewels embedded into it complemented it perfectly.

It was hard to believe I was staring back at myself in the mirror. With all this makeup on, I had to admit that I *was* beautiful. Yet the more I looked at my own figure, the deeper into my depression I sank.

"Just how long do you intend to wallow in your misery?"

"Father."

While I was busy scrutinizing myself in the mirror, my father entered the room with Ilia beside him. My clothes and makeup were all complete, so I was ready to go. My father had said something about us entering the hall together. The banquet had probably already begun...

I let out a long exhalation, when my father stared across at me. His shoulders drooped as he breathed a tired sigh. He seemed disappointed.

"Please just *try* to keep your mouth shut and conduct yourself like a royal princess..."

"Mind your own business! I've never even *considered* myself a princess!" I said in frustration.

My father raised an eyebrow. "Anis... Now isn't the time to let your mouth run away with you."

"...Very well, Father."

I breathed a sigh for what felt like the umpteenth time and flicked my mental switch.

I fought to calm my emotions, to take a bird's-eye view of the situation—to move outside myself and separate my mind from my heart.

Wearing a light smile, I bowed to my father. He stared back at me strangely, looking for all the world as though he had just seen a ghost. Normally, I would have pouted in response, but I maintained my smile as I took his hand.

"You should be careful not to let your subjects see you making such a face."

"...No matter how many times I see it, I'm always amazed that you can change your demeanor so quickly," my father said, truly impressed.

"I'm honored," I answered, bowing my head with a faint smile.

This was my princess mode, which I employed whenever I had to act as a royal for occasions like this. No matter what anyone said to me, I would smile softly and respond with perfect tranquility. This persona never failed to make my father deeply uncomfortable.

"Shall we be off? Thank you for escorting me, Father."

"...Hmm."

"We're going, Ilia."

"Yes, Your Highness. Take care."

As Ilia saw us off, I stepped into the banquet hall with my father by my side. The nobles in attendance had already arrived and were busy mingling and chatting among themselves.

The banquet was also a social gathering for the nobility. Attendance was necessary to take stock of all the latest information. *How many of them are truly happy that it was me who defeated the dragon?* I wondered as I made my way through the hall.

"All hail His Majesty King Orphans and Her Highness Princess Anisphia!"

The herald's announcement focused the room's attention on us as we entered the hall. I stretched my back to stand upright beside my dignified father.

First of all, my father would have to address the crowd, and so he made his way to the stage that had been prepared for such speeches before casting his gaze around at the gathered nobles.

"Thank you, everyone, for joining us this evening. Please make yourselves comfortable, as tonight is all about celebration. I've called the banquet after the recent dragon attack on our realm, which was forestalled by my unruly daughter, Anisphia."

With my father's introduction, I curtsied in the manner expected of a princess.

"Anisphia has accomplished a great feat, but she is not above censure, having acted at her own discretion. Nonetheless, this is not enough to outweigh such an achievement. As such, I have decided that she is owed an apt reward. On the other hand, my daughter was not alone in defeating the dragon on this occasion. Please welcome my loyal retainer, Duke Magenta, and his daughter, Euphyllia!"

Duke Grantz and Euphie both gave a reverent bow before joining us on the stage. Duke Grantz was dressed in an extravagant ceremonial dress, much more ornate than his usual attire.

And then there was Euphie. Her silvery-white hair was tied up in a bun, and she was wearing a dress colored in a gradient of blue shades. Her undisputed beauty was as radiant as the jewels she wore.

"My loyal vassal Euphyllia, daughter of Duke Grantz. I'm truly grateful that you accompanied my wayward daughter and took part in her effort to defeat the dragon threatening our lands."

"I'm honored, Your Majesty. I may be a young woman, but I am ready to stand on the battlefield whenever the realm is in danger. I must thank you for bestowing this honor on me in spite of my blunders and for appointing me as an assistant to Her Highness Princess Anisphia. I owe this honor to her—to your wonderful daughter," Euphie said, kneeling reverently.

I would normally feel incredibly embarrassed to have someone talk about me in this way, but for now, I fought to keep my emotions hidden.

"Hmm. I've caused you a fair amount of trouble, Euphyllia. My intention here isn't to try to make amends, but I do hope you will continue to show your loyalty by my unruly daughter's side."

"As you wish, Your Majesty."

"You've raised her well, Grantz. I hope I can rely on your continued support, too."

"My loyalty is always to the realm—and to you, Your Majesty."

Both Euphie and Duke Magenta gave my father perfect bows as they thanked him. My father nodded, glancing my way. At this signal, I turned fully toward him.

"Anisphia. Your achievement this time is nothing short of magnificent. But you have neglected your duties as a member of this royal household. I regret that I cannot praise you unreservedly. From now on, please conduct yourself in a manner more befitting of your station."

"I'll do my best to live up to the royal blood that flows through my veins."

"I trust that those words are true. Once again, you have done the realm a great service, Anisphia. As requested, the dragon magicite is yours. And while you won't be allowed to have all of them, you will also receive a share of the materials from the dragon's remains as well."

Yesss! I cheered in my heart, trying not to show my delight outwardly. Now the dragon's magicite crystal was mine! *Wow, I'm so happy! It was worth all that effort!*

My father cast another look at me, before turning his gaze to the nobles gathered in attendance. "As we all know, Anisphia's magicology research is to thank for resolving this great crisis. I hope she will continue to work for the benefit of the realm. Euphyllia?"

"Yes, Your Majesty?"

"Once more, I would like to ask you to continue to formally assist Anisphia."

"Understood. I would like to help Her Highness forge a righteous path."

"Hmm. Anisphia, the road ahead of you is yet unknown. Be sure not to tread wrong."

"I'll keep that in mind."

"Very well! In that case, everyone! Today we celebrate having averted this great crisis! I hope you enjoy the banquet!"

With my father's speech concluded, the rest of the party began to mill about once again, exchanging their thoughts. No sooner did I step down into the hall than a throng of nobles came to greet me. Euphie, Duke Grantz, and my father were similarly boxed in by the nobility.

Ah, I hate this! I hate having to do all this socializing! I forced myself to exchange pleasantries with a broad smile, all the while wondering how many of them were actually grateful for my success.

"Your Highness Princess Anisphia. Congratulations on your outstanding performance."

"Thank you. I'm afraid your praise is too much for me."

"Not at all. Allow me to introduce myself, Your Highness."

"Thank you for your kind words."

Wearing a smiling mask, I dealt with one noble after another as they came to greet me. Few, however, were willing to stay long enough to engage in real conversation. It was Euphie and my father who were speaking to their admirers at length. Both seemed to be enjoying whatever they were talking about.

I didn't normally attend these social gatherings. Everyone regarded me as an eccentric, I didn't have any interesting stories to discuss, and most of all, I was quite sure that some of these people didn't much like the fact that I was technically a member of the royal family.

I doubted very many of them would believe I'd had a change of heart and wanted to behave like royalty—and after all, what was done was done. The best course of action ahead of me would be to keep a low profile, at least until the situation with Allie was brought under control.

"Greetings, Princess Anisphia. I hope you're enjoying yourself?"

"Yes, thank you… Oh, Commander Sprout? Of the Royal Guard?"

I stared back at the acquaintance who had just called out to me. For a moment, the mask concealing my emotions slipped.

"It's been a while. I'm glad to see you're doing well," said the commander.

"It's a delight to speak with the honorable commander of the Royal Guard," I responded.

The prestigious Royal Guard was entrusted with the defense and protection of the Kingdom of Palettia's royal palace and its surrounding castle town. Among all the knightly orders, only the most elite warriors were selected to join.

The commander's name was Matthew Sprout, and in addition to leading the Royal Guard, he was also a count. He was the one who had taught me how to fight and use martial arts.

The commander was a mild-mannered man with dark-green hair and pale-green eyes, and he had the build of a well-trained warrior. Most of the time, he had a gentleness about him, but on the battlefield, he was simultaneously both a calm leader and a valiant warrior.

Due to his soft demeanor and abilities as a knight, he was a frequent target of the affections of the various maids of honor who worked at the royal palace—despite being married. Even now, I could feel the searing gazes of the ladies watching on from a distance.

"You're as popular as ever, I see," I remarked. "I'm envious."

"Are you teasing me, Princess Anisphia? You're very beautiful today in all your finery, aren't you?" Commander Sprout responded without breaking his smile.

At this comment, I felt the energy draining from my shoulders.

"I heard about your success on the battlefield. I must say that I would like to have a word with you about acting alone, but your efforts *have* kept casualties among the knights to a minimum. I believe I owe you my thanks."

"Not at all. I heard the situation was so grave that there was even talk of dispatching the Royal Guard. I'm just relieved that the knights who responded to the stampede didn't suffer any serious losses."

"I received a letter from them, by the way. They asked me to convey their gratitude to you."

"Well, please tell them that I'll keep on doing my utmost."

"Yes... So how was it? What was it like fighting a legendary dragon?" Commander Sprout asked, cutting to the heart of the matter with an unfaltering smile.

I straightened my back, staring back at him. "I'm glad I went. Regular knights would have been out of their element, if you ask me."

"Was it that strong?"

"It was the toughest opponent I've ever faced. I'm just glad I finished my Witch's Broom in time."

"Ah, I see. It must have been quite effective, both helping you get to the scene and to fight an airborne monster." The commander nodded, his keen gaze piercing. "Your magical tools truly are amazing, Princess Anisphia... But are you encountering trouble mass-producing them?"

My mask broke at that, and my smile turned bitter. "Thank you for saying so... But I'm not worthy of your praise, given the situation on that front."

"I'm afraid I don't follow... Although, I do sympathize."

Commander Sprout had been a great help in the development of my Mana Blades and in ensuring that they could be distributed to the maids working at the royal palace for their personal defense.

Above all, he understood the value of my magical tools and wanted to adopt them officially as equipment used by the knights. But at the same time, he also had a good understanding of internal politics within the kingdom, and of course, as the leader of the Royal Guard, he knew when not to overstep his bounds.

"I'm sure you caused His Majesty a good amount of trouble."

"Please continue to support my father."

"Oh? I wasn't expecting to hear that from you. In that case, would you consider devoting a bit more of your attention to social graces in the future?" the commander said with a forced smile.

Commander Sprout was around the same age as my father—and a good friend of his, too. If not for that, his suggestion would have struck me much harder, I'm sure.

"...And there's another matter I should mention. I must apologize in regard to what happened with Miss Euphyllia. There are no words adequate to express this, but please accept my deepest apologies." Commander Sprout bowed his head, his tone of voice having become unusually serious.

"Ah... You mean Navre? My sympathies, too."

The commander's son had been involved in the group who had arranged to break off Euphie's engagement.

I had heard that the commander was a good friend of Duke Grantz, and so he must have been shocked by the incident. He was a good person.

"There's no need for you to apologize, Commander Sprout. Besides, it was a good opportunity for me, too. And Euphie's help was essential in bringing down the dragon. It's because of that incident that we're here today, if I may say so. So everything turned out for the best. Please don't worry about it."

"...Thank you for saying that. Ah, this isn't really a conversation for a party, is it?"

"I don't mind at all."

"That's all I wanted to say, so thank you again… Ah, one more thing, Princess Anisphia. As the commander of the Royal Guard, I can't openly praise your actions. But I am truly grateful to have you looking out for the kingdom."

The commander met my eyes, then bowed deeply. All of a sudden, I found myself staring at his lowered head.

After a short moment, he looked back up at me, his expression curious, before he continued. "If not for you, a great many lives would have been lost. Despite the circumstances, I do sincerely hope you will one day take a more public-facing role."

"…You speak too highly of me, Commander Sprout."

"I wish you all the best in your future endeavors, great and small. Well then, I'll leave you to it."

"Thank you again."

The commander left with a warm, friendly smile. As I watched him leave, I let out a deep sigh. I was still somewhat nonplussed by that conversation.

…What a surprise. Commander Sprout was really singing my praises…

I was glad to hear that he thought so highly of me, but it was still difficult to accept.

Meanwhile, I realized that the music in the hall had changed to a dancing rhythm. Before I knew it, I was being asked by the sons of nobles to join them in the center of the hall.

I adopted an appropriate smile and tried my best not to let my ragged exhaustion show. If I made a misstep here, I would be the joke of the party.

Euphie and Ilia had given me special dancing lessons, but to be honest, the whole experience had been nothing if not traumatic. I would have to review everything on a regular basis to ensure I didn't forget…

After dancing with a couple of partners, I was starting to feel tired.

Maybe I should go to the balcony before someone else asks me…?

I quickly scurried off, the dancing music continuing behind me. Luckily, no one seemed to be following me. After making sure I was alone, I flicked the switch in my mind and let my princess mask fall. That act alone came as an enormous relief.

"...I'm no good at social gatherings."

Because I was a royal, my aversion to large events like this was a serious problem, but it was what it was. I had always been regarded as strange, and that was only a stone's throw away from being considered downright eccentric. The gazes directed my way were always probing, always harsh.

I just wanted to use magic. That was all. The second I had learned that magic existed, I hadn't been able to stop dreaming. So if I couldn't use magic the regular way, I would just have to find a new way. Because I *needed* magic, even if it meant breaking all the rules. If I could use it, I could bring smiles to people's faces. And then I could bring a smile to my own face, too. If I could do that, everyone would be happy.

"...I wish it was that easy."

Reality was cruel. What I had created was nowhere near the real thing, but at least I could actually call it magic. The problem was that *my* magic required breaking so many of the tenets that people took for granted, so it had never been truly accepted. Somewhere along the line, I had given up on studying magicology to help others. I had started to think that if I could make something for *me*, it would prove useful to others, too.

Only a handful of individuals truly understood me here. Maybe I could help them, I'd thought. So I had retreated to my villa in the detached palace. Of course, there were people who appreciated my inventions, like the commander of the Royal Guard. But not many. Few in this country were willing to accept my ideas.

"...I wish I could just study whatever I like..."

"Ah, Lady Anis! Here you are!"

"Waugh!"

I spun around at the sound of a voice calling out behind me. It was Euphie. We both leaned against the balcony, watching on as the banquet continued apace inside.

"Are you taking a break?"

"I can't do this. I'm no good at social gatherings. I've never liked them. How are *you* finding it, Euphie?"

Euphie raised her eyebrows in slight surprise at this question. She flashed me a vague smile, as though unsure how to respond. Then, lowering her gaze, she murmured, "…I'm pathetic. I acted like I knew what I was doing during your lessons, but the second a man's hand touches mine, I can't even breathe anymore…"

So that was it. She was still traumatized after what had happened with Allie. A bit of time had passed since then, but the wound must still have felt fresh. No wonder she found dancing with men painful.

All of a sudden, I realized she was holding her arms, trying to hide the fact that she was trembling slightly.

I reached out and took her hand. "Shall we dance, Euphie?"

"Huh? Together, Lady Anis?"

During my lessons, Euphie had played the role of the male dance partner, so I knew she was fully capable of dancing. Of course, it wouldn't be appropriate for two young women to dance together in public. That must have been why she looked so perplexed by my invitation.

Still, I held her hand in my own. "There aren't many people here, certainly no one who would hold it against us. And I know you like dancing. So it would be such a waste not to."

"…It would?"

Euphie gave me a small smile, blinking in surprise, then accepted my hand. Once she was ready, I began to take the lead.

We danced together in perfect harmony, just as she had taught me, albeit our roles reversed. Thinking how strange it was, I couldn't help but grin—and Euphie smiled back.

We danced hand in hand on the balcony, away from the glamour of the celebrations. I couldn't help but smile when I considered how surprising this must look to anyone watching. I wasn't sure if Euphie felt the same way, but she let out a soft murmur: "…We must look so absurd dancing together."

"All that matters is that we're enjoying ourselves, right?"

"If our fathers could see us, they would be aghast."

"Let them! What good is dancing if you don't enjoy it?!"

We followed the steps, spinning around together. At that moment, the music came to a stop, and there was a brief silence before the next song got underway. But Euphie didn't let go of my hand. Our gazes met, our hands still intertwined. She was staring straight into me.

"...I sometimes wonder, what would have happened if you hadn't taken me away that day... I would have cried, I would have been crushed, I would have hated everything... I'm sure of it... I would have been broken inside."

"...Yeah."

"But you saved me from all that. Now I can put it all into words. I was so happy, Lady Anis. Thank you so much for giving me a chance after I had failed at everything else."

"Yeah."

"I'm sure you'll keep on slaying dragons and doing other ridiculous things. And I know you're no good at these social events. So I'll help supplement your weaknesses."

"...Euphie."

Out of nowhere, the moon shone through a break in the clouds, illuminating her face as she gazed into my eyes. Her silver-white hair, glimmering in the moonlight, shook slightly in the night breeze.

"You're so important to me. I can't take my eyes off you. I want to stay with you," Euphie said with a smile as she intertwined her fingers through mine.

Her smile was mesmerizing. I couldn't look away.

My magic existed to make people smile—if I could do that, my childhood dream would come true. As I had grown older, that dream had come to seem distant and cold.

I could only reach so far by myself, so I swore to myself not to let go of this hand linked with mine. This was the happiness I had always wanted. That feeling was like a comforting fire in my chest.

When this boring party was over, we would have more time. Time to figure out what we didn't yet understand. There were still new sights to see, new creations to give form.

And—I wanted to enjoy life here in this world.

I was holding hands with someone I truly cared about. The kind of magic user I had always wanted to be. She was perfect, my lifelong ideal, and she was holding my hand now. She had accepted me. She had told me there was nothing wrong with my magic.

It felt like being forgiven. I could follow this path. I had always put on a brave face, always acted as though I didn't need anyone's approval. I was used to walking by myself despite the rejection.

But maybe, just maybe, with Euphie by my side, I could accomplish all those things I hadn't been able to do on my own. Maybe I wouldn't need to smother the passions of my heart anymore.

I was embarrassed to acknowledge these uncertain feelings, and I shook my head trying to dispel them. Then I gave my partner a heartfelt smile.

"Don't leave me, Euphie! There's still so much more to do!"

AFTERWORD

When I think about girls who can use magic, it's an image of a young witch flying on a broomstick that initially comes to mind.

To my first-time readers, it's a pleasure to meet you. To those of you who have read my web novel, I truly appreciate your continued support. I'm Piero Karasu.

Thank you so much for taking the time to read *The Magical Revolution of the Reincarnated Princess and the Genius Young Lady*. I've reworked the story somewhat for this print edition. How did you like it?

In pursuit of my dream to become a novelist, I originally serialized this tale online under the title *The Reincarnated Princess Still Yearns for Magic*, and while the general outline remains unchanged, the contents have been revised considerably. If you've read both versions, I hope you've enjoyed spotting the differences.

With a great deal of help from my editor, we revised the print version starting from when Anisphia and Euphyllia first meet, until we settled on the book's current form. There were things I couldn't depict well before and others that only came to light during the revision process, so I really focused on incorporating them all into this volume.

As a writer, it's my job to send a prototype of a work out into the world, but I also believe it is the voices of everyone else involved in the project who help give it color. Now that I've been able to work with my team on this story, I hold that sentiment even more strongly.

The power of illustrations is truly amazing. Some aspects of the setting were rather difficult to imagine or convey in prose, and I felt that the pictures helped to express them quite effectively.

While I might have written the original work, it's thanks to those images that I've been able to produce a much stronger visual interpretation of the world of the story. I would like to take this opportunity to express my gratitude to Yuri Kisaragi once again for the illustrations.

I would also like to express my sincerest thanks to my editor for giving me the opportunity to publish the first volume of the story, based on the first chapter of the web version, focusing on how Anisphia and Euphyllia come to meet and ending with the two of them holding hands after a dance at the banquet.

Thank you to everyone who gave this work a chance. I truly hope that this book adds a little color to your lives. Hopefully I'll see you again with the next volume. Until then.

Piero Karasu